BOOKED

A RYLIE COOPER MYSTERY

STELLA BIXBY

FERRY TAIL PUBLISHING LLC

For all my mystery author friends - I hope your fictional murders never come to fruition!

1

The moon shone over the lake.

The killer was close. I could feel it deep in my bones. It was like the ache I got in my shoulder every time a thunderstorm started rolling in.

"I didn't expect to see you here, Tiffany," a man's voice came from around the corner of the cabin.

I steadied myself as best I could.

"Come on out. You've been caught."

When the man stepped into the moonlight, my breath caught in my chest. "It was you? How could it be you?" I hated how my voice sounded—like that of a whiny child. "You're supposed to be one of the good ones."

"I am one of the good ones."

"Why did you do it?" I asked.

"You know why," he said, looking down the driveway as if expecting someone.

"You said you'd moved past it," I said. How had I been so stupid to believe him?

"I have," he said, turning his attention back to me. "Well, now I have."

"She'll never forgive you. You'll never get her back."

"That's not what I was trying to do." He took a step toward me, but I stepped away. "I don't care about her anymore."

"Then why did you kill the man she left you for? If you were over it, you wouldn't need to kill him. Or anyone."

His face showed no remorse. "I need to get out of here. If you found me, the police will be right behind you. In fact, I'm surprised they didn't beat you to it."

"What's that supposed to mean?" I asked.

He didn't answer.

Instead, he pulled a gun from the holster on his hip.

But I was faster.

I took the shot I never thought I'd have to take.

His arm wasn't even parallel with the ground before my bullet found purchase, and he fell backward toward the water.

Police rushed in behind me as tears streamed down my face.

"You did what you had to do," one of them said. But all I could think about was how he and I had spent so many hours together working on cases. He'd been my best friend.

I closed the book and sighed. Henrietta Rose was masterful.

I'd always hated reading until I picked up one of her books. Now, I could hardly wait to read the next one.

"Wanna go for a walk?" I asked Fizzy, my pit bull Lab mix.

He flew off the couch and started jumping like he had springs in his back legs.

"I'll take that as a yes." I thought about how Garrett and I used to take Fizzy and Babbitt on walks together most nights but pushed the thought away. It was no use dwelling on the past.

The evening spring air was enough to elicit a chill and necessitate a jacket. I grabbed my favorite Denver Broncos hoodie and locked the door behind me.

Only a few steps from my apartment building, my phone rang. "Hello?"

"Rylie? Are you there?" My mom sounded like she was in a gymnasium with all the noise behind her.

"Yep, I'm here. Where are you?"

"Your sister and I just finished our pickleball game. We beat them by a landslide."

I didn't have the heart to remind her that the people she played against were easily twenty years older than her and more than twice my sister's age. "That's great."

"I wanted to invite you over for dinner tonight," she said. "It's been a while since we had a family dinner, and I'm missing my girl."

"Can't tonight," I said. "I have plans. But I'll come over soon."

"You've been saying that for weeks. Did I do something wrong? What can I change to make you want to spend time with me again?"

"I've been super busy since I returned from Ireland." I'd visited Ireland to see my best friend and roommate—Shayla—who had recently decided she wasn't coming back to the United States. I guess that made her my ex-roommate.

I pushed the thought away so I wouldn't start crying . . . again.

"Busy doing what?" Mom asked. Of course, she wouldn't let this go. "Reading those ridiculous mystery novels."

"They're not ridiculous," I said. "They're fun."

"I tried to read one, and it was so far-fetched I had to put it down."

I did my best not to get irritated as we turned down a side street toward the park where Fizzy liked to roll in the mud. "Well, I like them."

"You know, you can't just sit around reading silly mysteries for the rest of your life. You're going to have to go back to work. Or get another job if being a park ranger isn't what you want to do."

When I'd returned from my groom-free honeymoon just before Christmas, I had been sure I wanted to go back. I told my boss—Ursula—that I'd be back after my Ireland trip.

Since then, I'd pushed the timeline out approximately ten or eleven times. It was only a matter of time before she gave me an ultimatum . . . or gave up.

Without a roommate or a job, making my bills wasn't easy—my savings was nearly all gone. Thankfully, I was good friends with my landlord, my car had been paid in full, and I didn't mind eating ramen most nights of the week.

"I'll get a job," I said. "Or go back to the reservoir. I don't know yet."

Mom sighed into the receiver loudly enough for her entire gym to hear it. Even Fizzy glanced up at me with a look of worry in his eye. "I'll call you next week about dinner. Try not to make any plans."

We said our goodbyes and disconnected the call. As Fizzy rolled in the mud, I scrolled through the newest video app that was all the hype with the younger kids. It was only a matter of time before people my age made it uncool.

I shook my head. Since when was I old enough to make something uncool?

"Stuck in a rut?" A woman with pretty brown hair and big eyes smiled at me from my phone. "Revamp your life in six days."

I was about to swipe to the next video, but something stopped me.

"Day One: Purge. Get rid of anything you don't absolutely adore. Is your ex's stuff still hiding in your closet? Burn it or return it."

I chuckled a bit at her rhyme.

"Day Two: Get out of the house. Go on a date. Or to dinner with friends. No, your dog doesn't count."

I glanced at Fizzy, who was happily running through the dog park.

"Day Three: Get a new pet. You heard me—a NEW pet. Don't get rid of your old pet. Just get another pet. Someone new to liven up your place."

Fizzy was lively enough. I shook my head at the thought of this.

"Day Four: Redecorate. Splurge on yourself. Make your

space a place you're eager to come home to after a long day of work."

My stomach turned at the thought of a long day of work. Not because I was lazy but because I couldn't see myself returning to the reservoir without Shayla or Luke working somewhere in the city. What if I found a dead body? I'd need one of them to help me with the crime scene. Okay, fine, there were other officers I trusted, but Shayla and Luke were police officers *and* my friends.

At least, I thought Luke was still my friend after the falling out we had at Christmas.

The video had come to the end and was now replaying. I had no way of fast-forwarding. I'd have to watch it again to get to days five and six.

I watched Fizzy roll in another mud puddle before I heard the pretty brunette say, "Day Five: Try a new activity. Pretty simple, right? And Day Six: Have a big party to celebrate your revamped lifestyle. Follow me for more tips."

I hit the follow button and saved the video. Maybe my life did need a little revamping.

2

D ay one was a breeze. Cleaning everything out
of the apartment really meant my bedroom
since Shayla had already had her belongings
packed up and shipped to Ireland.

Her door stayed closed. It hurt too much to look in
there and see an empty space where my best friend used
to be. It was like a physical representation of the hole in
my heart.

I only had a few of Garrett's things still in my closet.
Things I hadn't realized had been there.

Part of me wanted to burn them, but the other part
knew that wasn't the right thing to do. I loaded them into
the trunk of my red Mustang convertible—Cherry Anne
the Second—and headed toward his house.

I hadn't been in Garrett's neighborhood since I'd
collected my things after our wedding fell apart. Garrett
hadn't been there. In fact, I hadn't seen him since he
walked back down the aisle without my hand in his.

The house looked the same as it always had—a two-story brick home in the nicest part of town. The garage doors were closed, and—if Garrett was home—both his truck and his car were parked inside.

I sucked in a breath, pulled the box from my trunk, and walked up the steps to the front door.

When I knocked, Babbitt barked a few times.

"Oh, Babbitt, it's just a nice lady." A woman I'd never seen before wearing a long skirt and fitted blouse opened the door. "Can I help you with something?"

My heart pounded too loudly for my brain to put words together. Was this perhaps his sister? The last time I saw a woman at his door and had suspected something else, it had been his mother.

"Are you his sister?" I asked.

She giggled a bit. "No, I'm his fiancée." She held up a ring that looked slightly larger than the one Garrett had given me. At least he hadn't used the same one.

"I—uh—" I tried to make out the words, but nothing would come.

"You look like you might pass out. Do you want to come in? I can get you some water."

I shook my head furiously. "This. Garrett's. Stuff." I practically threw the box at her and turned to run.

Too bad my feet didn't get the memo.

My body turned, but my feet stayed put, causing me to topple down the top three steps onto the steep hill.

"Oh my goodness," Garrett's fiancée said, hurrying to help me.

Babbitt came to my side and started licking the tears leaking from my eyes.

"Can I help you up?" the woman asked. "Garrett should be home from work soon if you need to talk to him."

I hugged Babbitt around the neck, then brought myself to a stand. "I'm okay," I said. "Just let Garrett know Rylie stopped by to drop off the last of his stuff."

Her eyes widened in recognition. At least he'd talked about me.

Before she could say anything, I stood and marched down the steps with as much dignity as I had left.

"It was nice to meet you, Rylie," the woman said.

I lifted a hand and waved without looking back at her.

Who was that ridiculous woman on that ridiculous app to tell me how to revamp my life? She was probably just some stupid influencer who roped people in with false promises and six-day plans that didn't even work.

I sat in my living room and opened the app, heading straight to her profile.

She had one point seven million followers and was listed as a licensed life coach with the little check mark that said she was legit.

Psh, what did an app know about who was legit?

As I scrolled through her videos, she was side by side with other people's videos who talked about how her six-day program changed their lives.

None of them talked about nearly quitting on day one. Maybe I was just a wimp. Maybe day two would be better.

I watched the video again to remind myself what day two was all about.

"Get out of the house. Go on a date. Or to dinner with friends. No, your dog doesn't count."

The only friends I had were the rangers. If I went to dinner with them, they'd inevitably ask when I was coming back. That was a no-go. My mother's offer tickled the back of my mind, but I quickly pushed it away. She said a date or friends. Not family.

Where would I find a date on such short notice?

I swiped through the app, trying to think of something. Or maybe think of nothing. About three videos in, an ad popped up for a new dating app called Just Personalities. No pictures. Just your personality.

Maybe that's what I needed—to fall for someone because of their personality instead of their looks. All the guys I'd dated or been attracted to since high school were the overly gorgeous types. Maybe I needed to go for someone because of their mind instead.

I clicked on the button to join. What did I have to lose?

The first thing it asked for was my name, then my favorite foods, my favorite tv shows, and a few other favorites. Then it asked me to create a short bio.

I tried to remember what Shayla had written about me on the app that had eventually—in a roundabout way—introduced me to Garrett. The thought of Shayla and me trying to put together my profile made me teary-eyed.

I ended up settling on: *Loves Burgers, Beer, and the Broncos.*

It was all I could think of.

Now, I had to wait to see who I might be compatible with.

I put the phone on the coffee table and went to the kitchen to make myself a microwaved quesadilla. It wasn't much, but it was cheap and delicious.

My phone pinged, and I practically dove over the couch to see if it was a notification from the app.

It wasn't.

A message from Ursula said:

Need an answer. Could really use your help.

I felt like I was being sucked into a massive vacuum cleaner by my ass. What could I possibly say?

I need more time.

Her reply was almost immediate.

We need your help now.

Why? What's going on?

That's classified unless you're willing to commit to returning.

I put the phone down. As curious as I was, I wouldn't give in to her manipulation. It was slightly hilarious—or ironic—that she was so adamant about me coming back when she'd been the one who threatened to fire me several times at the beginning of my employment.

She could wait for an answer. And if she couldn't, she could just find someone to replace me.

I picked up the next book in the mystery series and started reading.

3

fter staying up all night to finish the book, I needed a nap and a shower. Preferably in that order.

When my phone rang just as my consciousness faded, I almost pushed the ignore button. But it was Nikki, and she rarely called me.

"What's up?" I asked, keeping my voice intentionally groggy so maybe she'd get the hint.

"Are you still sleeping?" Nikki asked, disgust in her voice.

"I just went to bed," I said. "I was up reading all night."

"Do you have just a couple of minutes to listen? And maybe give me your input?"

I sat up so I wouldn't fall asleep while on the phone with her. "Sure."

"You cannot tell anyone I'm telling you this," she said. "It's just, I'm stuck, and the only person I can think to talk to about it is you."

"Is everything okay?" I asked. "Are you pregnant with Naked Guy's baby?"

"His name is Oliver," Nikki said, "and I'm not pregnant. This is about a case I've been working on."

That made sense why she didn't want me to tell anyone. This was probably the leverage Ursula was trying to use to get me to come back. "Okay, spill. I won't say anything."

"Rylie," Nikki's voice hushed slightly and became more serious, "there have been four murders in the last month in Prairie City parks."

I sat up straighter. "Four?"

"All single men in their mid to late forties," Nikki continued. "And we can't find a connection. There hasn't been a murder at one of the parks since the boat explosion months ago."

"And now there have been four in a month," I said. "That's not great. How did they die?"

It sounded like Nikki was shuffling papers in the background. "We found the first guy in a floating barrel at Alder Ridge. The forensic team believes someone put him in the barrel with an acid mixture before throwing the barrel and all its contents into the water."

Just the thought made my skin crawl. "Sounds horrible."

"The second looked like a suicide by gunshot, but the gun was missing," Nikki said. "When we looked into it more closely, we realized it was definitely a murder."

The hairs on the back of my neck rose. It couldn't be. It had to be a coincidence.

"The third was on the bike path where a runner

stepped on a buried explosive and blew up."

That was it. I knew what was happening. "Are there any cabins in Prairie City parks?"

Nikki didn't reply for a few seconds. "Why do you ask that?"

"I'm going to take a wild guess here," I said. "You found the next guy in a cabin that had been set on fire, but he didn't die from the fire. He died from poisoning."

Nikki was silent.

"Have the news stations reported on these murders?" Surely someone else would have come up with this theory before me.

"We've kept them out," Nikki said. "But how did you—"

"They're murders based on books," I said. "Henrietta Rose's Black is the New Dead Series. You basically outlined every murder in the first four books."

"Except we haven't gotten toxicology reports back from the guy in the cabin," Nikki said. "We assumed he died from smoke inhalation."

"It happened like that in the book, too," I said. "It's okay. You can't know until you get the reports."

"Rylie, this is big," Nikki said. "I need your help with this. Please come back and help me?"

"The next book had a guy who was suffocated, then taken to a lake and thrown in, so it looked like he drowned," I said. "You should keep an eye out at the lakes for whoever is doing this."

"Please," Nikki asked.

"Sorry," I said. "I can't. It's too soon."

Nikki said nothing for what felt like forever.

I finally had to break the silence. "If that's it, I need to get some rest."

"Yep," Nikki said. "Bye."

She hung up before I could say anything.

I fell asleep within seconds of my head hitting the pillow.

When Fizzy started barking like a crazy person, it took everything in me not to yell at him.

"Fizzy, stop," I said. "I'm tired. I've only had a little bit of sleep. We'll go on a walk in a little while."

He wouldn't stop.

"Fine," I said. "But this better be important."

I followed him to the living room and realized someone was knocking on the door.

I glanced at my reflection in the mirror, but I could hardly see myself. I flipped on the light and straightened my hair before answering.

Detective Harry Bryant of the Prairie City Police Department and Nikki stood on the other side of the door. They both looked extra official, with Harry in his uniform and Nikki in a polo and khaki pants that took nothing away from her model-like physique.

"What's going on? Did something happen?" Panic rushed through me. They'd only be at my door—together —if something terrible had happened. "Is it my mom? My dad? My sister?"

"No, nothing like that," Harry said. "I believe Ursula texted you and told you we needed your help?"

Nikki gave me a slightly panicked look. No matter how irritated I was with their persistence, I wouldn't rat her out. We may have started off as enemies, but we'd become something like friends.

"I didn't agree to help," I said.

"That's why Ursula sent us over," Nikki said. "Because you're being a stubborn recluse."

"I'm just taking some time to—"

"Wallow in self-pity?" Nikki shook her head. "When's the last time you left the house?"

"I took Fizzy on a walk yesterday," I said. "We'll go on another one tonight."

"Tonight? In the dark?" Nikki pointed to the window.

I hadn't realized it was already dark outside. I'd slept all day.

"Ursula didn't want us to discuss this with you unless you agreed to come back, but we know you can keep things confidential and won't share what we tell you."

I had to play this like I didn't already know what he was about to tell me. But I also didn't really want to be part of the case. "Please don't tell me. I'm sure you can figure it out on your own."

Nikki shuffled her feet and tucked her long auburn hair behind her ear. I'd already given her the key to solving it. All she had to do was figure out who was copying Henrietta Rose's books.

"Rylie," Harry said in a low father-type voice. "I wouldn't be here if it wasn't important. We need a fresh set of eyes on this. At least let me tell you what we're dealing with."

He used to hate me. He'd tried to get me fired and had

me kicked off of cases. Now he wanted my help.

Nikki and I had been enemies. Now we were friends.

Ursula didn't think I'd last a single summer. Now she was practically begging me to come back.

Maybe Shayla and Luke and Garrett had left me and moved on, but people still cared.

"Okay, you can tell me about it," I said. "But I make no promises."

Nikki smiled and sat in the chair across the coffee table from me.

Harry pulled a file folder from the briefcase he'd brought with him. "We've had four murders on Prairie City properties in the last month."

I tried to act surprised. "Four? That's a lot."

"I guess you're not the shit magnet after all," Nikki said.

I rolled my eyes at her. "Do you think they're connected?"

Harry shook his head. "We can't tell. Nothing we've come up with connects them other than that they're all men in their mid to late forties."

"Were they all killed in the same way?"

Harry opened the file, then stopped. "These are pretty gruesome. Do you think you can stomach them?"

I nodded. "I haven't eaten in twenty-four hours." As if on cue, my stomach growled.

"You might want to eat before seeing these because you'll likely lose your appetite afterward."

"I'm okay," I said. "Just show me."

He wasn't lying. The pictures were not pretty.

"We found this man in a barrel that floated up in the

middle of the reservoir. We think he was put in this barrel with acid." Harry pointed to the photograph of a man who was barely distinguishable as a human at all.

"Any fingerprints or DNA?" I asked.

"Nothing," he said.

"This one looks like a suicide, but they ended up ruling it a murder," Nikki said. "The gunshot wound would have left residue and burns on his skin but didn't, meaning someone else shot him from farther away. Also, the gun was never recovered."

I sucked in a breath and moved my gaze to the next photo. "Oh my gosh." I averted my gaze. Why hadn't I thought of what was coming?

"This man stepped on a bomb under the crusher fine on the running trail. The bomb was powerful enough to blow up an entire building." Harry turned the page. "This one died from smoke inhalation."

"Are you sure?" I asked.

Nikki cleared her throat. "They found him inside a burning cabin."

"I didn't know we had cabins in the parks," I said, trying to cover up the fact that I'd almost blown Nikki's cover.

"It's one of the old ones up on the newly acquired property in the foothills," Nikki said. "It's been scheduled for teardown for a while."

"Can you think of anything that might tie these together?" Harry finally asked.

I glanced from him to Nikki. She gave me a slight nod.

"These are copycat murders," I said. "It looks like you have a serial killer on your hands."

4

Harry stared at me for longer than was necessary while Nikki shifted in her seat, waiting for me to tell Harry everything I'd already told her.

"Here." I stood and walked to my small bookshelf. "It'll be easier to show you than tell you." I took the first four books in the Black is the New Dead Series by Henrietta Rose off my shelf and handed them to Harry.

"Can you, uh, explain?" Harry's tone was gentle, almost like he thought I was going insane.

"Those murders—all four of them—are in the first four books of this series," I said. "Did you give them to me in the order they occurred?"

Nikki nodded.

"That's the order they were in the books, too." I took the books and glanced at the back of the first. "Acid barrel." I handed it to him and moved on to the second. "Suicide set up." I set the second on top of the first in his lap. "Runner steps on a bomb." I handed Nikki the third.

"And poisoning in a remote cabin." I waved the fourth book in the air. "Granted, you probably haven't gotten the toxicology reports back yet. But you'll see he didn't die from the fire."

They sat in silence.

Harry's expression changed from skepticism to horror. "Are there any other books in the series?"

I jogged to my bedroom—Fizzy following me, barking loudly—and returned with the novel I'd completed in the wee hours of the morning.

"This is the most recent release," I said, handing the book to Harry. "Someone dies by suffocation, but it looks like they died by accidental drowning until they find a note on the body. It's a puzzle the sleuth has to figure out to find the killer."

Harry took the book from me and flipped through the pages.

"Is there a rhythm to the murders? Like a time between them? Maybe it correlates to the time between the books being published." I looked from Harry to Nikki.

"Were they not all published on a schedule?" Nikki asked.

I shook my head. "She's an independent publisher, so she publishes whenever she gets the book done." I pulled out my phone to check a retail site with the release dates. "Book two came out about two months after book one, book three about four months after book two, book four about three months after book three, book five released about a month ago, and the sixth book is supposed to release next week—a month after book five."

I could see Harry doing the math in his head before he

shook it. "It's a good theory, but it doesn't line up. As far as we can tell, each of the murders has happened about a week apart."

"How long ago was the last murder?" I asked.

"About a week ago," Nikki said. "Which means—"

"The suffocation drowning could be happening as we speak," I finished.

It took less than two minutes to pull on jeans and a hoodie. Harry was on the phone with dispatch, trying to get every officer available to any local parks with water features.

Nikki drove the three of us to the Alder Ridge Reservoir in her big, black ranger truck. As we pulled up to the gate where Antonio—one of the other rangers—stood looking like he'd just stepped off the cover of Italian Vogue, my chest swelled.

Pulling up to the reservoir felt like coming home after a long vacation. The trees lining the side of the road seemed to wave in greeting as the late-night breeze wound through their branches.

"We'll head to the back gates," Nikki told Antonio. "Watch the plaza area."

"If you see anything, call us," Harry said. "We don't know what this person is capable of."

Antonio and Harry were friends from way back. Antonio nodded, but his gaze never left me.

"It is so nice to see you back," Antonio said, his voice a low Italian rumble. "I—we—missed you."

"Let's catch up with Rylie later," Nikki said. "We have a killer to stop."

She pulled through the gate, and it took everything in me not to turn back to see if Antonio was watching us leave.

He'd been at my wedding along with the other rangers. They'd navigated the great snowstorm and sat there to support me. And they'd been there to dance and drink the night away at my reception when everything fell apart.

But eventually, they'd stopped calling when I stopped answering. Every once in a while, I'd get a text from Ben or Greg or Nikki, but Antonio kept his distance. Maybe now that I was single again, he wanted to stay away from me. He seemed to have a thing for unavailable women.

5

The moon hung bright over the reservoir, casting eerie shadows along the banks. We tore around the bike path like it was a NASCAR road course. Each walk-in gate we passed was free from movement or cars parked outside on the street.

I tried to remember the details of the book. The man had been found floating in the water and looked like he'd drowned accidentally, but no water was in his lungs, meaning he'd been suffocated before drowning. If that were the case, there would have to be drag marks unless the killer was strong enough to carry the dead weight of a forty-year-old man.

It was so surreal practically living the book I'd read less than twenty-four hours before.

As we turned the corner to the last walk-in gate, Antonio came on the radio. "Ranger Four, Ranger Five."

It caught me off guard before I remembered everyone changed numbers now that Seamus wasn't returning.

Which would mean I'd be Ranger Six. I cleared my throat to fight the tears that threatened to come as I thought about Seamus and Shayla not coming back.

Nikki clicked the mic on her shoulder and said, "Go ahead."

"I have movement on the swim beach," Antonio said. "It's at least one person, if not two. I'm going to get closer."

"Tell him to wait," Harry said. "We're almost there."

"Standby, Ranger Four," Nikki said. "We'll be there in two minutes."

She gunned the accelerator and turned so sharply that I felt like my body was crushing in on itself against the car door.

Antonio didn't reply to Nikki's instructions.

"Ranger Four, did you copy?"

No reply.

If I knew Antonio, he wasn't about to let someone drown right in front of him while he waited for backup.

When we came around the last turn leading us to the main plaza area, I could barely see two figures running across the sand—one chasing the other.

"Antonio's chasing someone," I said. "We have to help him. What if they have a gun?"

Nikki said nothing before turning the truck's wheel, hopping the curb, and driving straight through the plaza past the thatched roof, tiki-style buildings.

We lost sight of them for a second but came out where they should have ended up—in the boat ramp parking lot. However, when we got there, Antonio stood alone, looking around frantically as if the other person had simply disappeared.

"Where'd they go?" Harry said, jumping out of the truck before it even stopped.

"I—I don't know," Antonio said through deep breaths. "I came around the corner, and they were just gone."

"Did you get a look at their face? Was it a man, a woman? Anything?" Harry asked.

Antonio shook his head. "I just saw them in the water. I yelled and took off after them."

Nikki and I exchanged glances, and both jumped back into the truck. "Let's go check the water," she said.

Antonio and Harry jumped into the bed, and she tore down the beach toward the cordoned-off area where—during the summer—kids splashed, and people swam laps to prepare them for the open water swim portion of a triathlon.

"There," Antonio shouted from the back. "On the far end, something's floating."

When Nikki came to a stop, it was apparent what was floating.

Antonio was the first to jump in, splashing through the freezing cold water toward the body.

He and Harry pulled the small man out and laid him on the beach before starting CPR.

Nikki switched her radio and called dispatch to get an ambulance on the way.

"I can open the gate for them," I said.

Nikki nodded. "Take the truck."

I hopped in the driver's side and sped toward the main entrance gate. The ambulance likely wouldn't arrive for a few minutes, but I wanted to beat them there just in case they were in the area. Nothing was worse than making the ambulance wait behind a locked gate.

The ambulance arrived within minutes of me opening the gate. I gave them quick directions before they headed toward the plaza.

Part of me wanted to leave the gate open and go back to the plaza to see if I could help, but leaving the gate open during off hours was a recipe for disaster. If someone came in and we locked them inside, Ursula would likely rescind her offer for me to come back.

And after tonight, I was definitely coming back.

6

As I stood impatiently next to the gate, I watched a couple of cars drive by on the main road off the park entrance road. I tried to see the stars, but the clouds had come in, making the once bright moonlit sky misty and dark.

I turned my attention back down the road leading to the plaza, anticipating the ambulance's lights to crest the hill at any moment. But instead of lights, I saw what looked like the figure of someone sneaking through the brush on the hillside.

I didn't have a radio, so I couldn't call out to Antonio or Nikki. But even if I did, they didn't have the truck. I did.

Did I stay with the open gate or go after the person who likely had just tried to drown someone?

And if I went after them, did I leave the gate open?

It was an impossible situation, but I went with my gut.

I left the gate open with the truck angled out of the

way so the ambulance could get by, then I took off as quickly and quietly as possible.

At first, it seemed like the person didn't see me. They were still sneaking methodically through the grass.

I used this to my advantage and ran faster.

I was almost to them when I tripped on something hard and fell to the ground.

Hard.

When I glanced up, I saw the person running in the distance. There was no way I'd catch them now.

I hurried to where I thought I'd seen them and pulled out my phone, opening the flashlight app and searching the ground where they'd walked.

The light of my flashlight finally washed over what looked like child-sized footprints in the dirt. I searched for other footprints but found none. Those had to belong to the person I'd seen running.

There was a definite possibility that whoever I'd seen wasn't the same person as Antonio had chased off the beach—people came into the reservoir unauthorized at night all the time. But no matter how much I searched for anything else that might connect this person to the person on the beach, I came up empty-handed.

I sighed and jogged back to the truck just as the ambulance lights came over the hill.

I waved as they passed and locked the gate behind them.

When I parked the truck in the ranger parking area next to the plaza, Antonio, Harry, and Nikki greeted me with sad expressions.

"Did he die?" I asked, hopping out of the truck.

"He's dead," Nikki said.

Harry kicked the ground. "How did I not see the book connection? We might have caught on more quickly if I had allowed the media some information. I mean, even I know who Henrietta Rose is, and I don't read mysteries."

"You don't read mysteries?" I asked.

"I have enough crime in my daily life," he said. "I'm more of a romance guy."

Nikki chuckled a bit.

"What?" Harry said. "There's nothing wrong with a man who reads romance. It keeps my wife awfully happy. What do you read?"

Nikki stopped laughing. "I don't read."

"Well, you should," Harry said. "It makes you smarter."

"I saw someone running out by the gate," I said. "I tried to go after them, but I fell, and they got away. Their footprints were really small, so it's possible it was a child and not the same person at all."

"Can you remember anything about what the person you chased looked like?" Harry asked Antonio.

"I am sorry," Antonio said. "They seemed to be simply watching the body float in the water when I got to them, but they bolted the minute they saw me. I believe they were smaller—around Rylie's size, maybe a few inches shorter—and very fast."

Something about him calling me small made my cheeks flame. Usually, my sister was the one people called small since she was practically a twig. I was taller and had a much more athletic build, even though she was the one who participated in marathons and triathlons and toddler taming.

"The man you pulled from the water was relatively small himself," Nikki said. "Do you think the killer could have drowned him here?"

"Were there drag marks in the sand?" I asked.

"Nothing that looked like a body had been dragged from the parking lot . . . or from anywhere, for that matter." Nikki glanced around as if she might spot a vehicle we hadn't previously seen.

"Which means the man likely entered with his killer willingly," I said. "But that's not how it happened in the books. There were drag marks in the books."

"Maybe the killer drugged him once they got down there?" Harry said. "Or they could be stronger than someone their size normally is. I know some little guys who could drop a three-hundred-pound man in a matter of seconds."

"Did you look between his butt cheeks for the puzzle?" I asked.

Antonio glanced at me like I'd gone crazy.

Nikki and Harry burst out laughing.

"This is not a time to laugh," I said, unable to keep myself from chuckling slightly.

"You didn't tell us we had to look between his butt cheeks," Nikki finally said.

"We checked his pockets," Harry said, "his waistband and collar."

"It wasn't in his clothes," I said. "It was between his butt cheeks."

"I rarely check between someone's butt cheeks when

I'm giving them CPR," Harry said. "But we can call the hospital and ask."

I raised my eyebrows.

"Now," Harry said. "I'll call them now."

He pulled out his phone and walked away from us, probably because of the ridiculousness of his request and the fact that Antonio and Nikki were still giggling like schoolgirls.

When Harry returned, he smiled. "They found an encrypted note—the puzzle—between his butt cheeks." He shook his head. "They're going to send a photo to my email."

"Let's go in the office, and we can try to figure it out," I said, stifling a yawn. It was going to be another long night.

No matter how often we read the note or compared it to the cipher in the book, we couldn't make sense of it. This meant the killer was willing to go off script a bit to do what they wanted.

"Maybe one of the officers at the station can work on this," Harry said. "A couple of them are good at these sorts of things."

He emailed a picture of the note to a few of his colleagues.

"We could always ask the author," I said. "In fact, we should probably talk to her to see what's in her next book so we can head off the next murder before the book is released."

"When does the next book release?" Harry asked.

"Five days," I said.

"That means we don't have much time," Nikki said. "Maybe the author is the murderer."

I gasped.

"What?" Nikki asked. "She knows these murders by

heart. She likely researched how to kill people, and no one would suspect her because it would be too obvious."

I wanted to tell her off. This was my favorite author she was talking about. I mean, she was the only author I'd read outside of mandatory school books but still. Henrietta was probably the nicest person on the planet who just liked to write a good mystery for the fun of it.

"Why don't we pay her a visit so she can clear all of this up?" I asked. "She lives around here. We just need to find out where."

"I think we should talk to her," Harry said. "If only for the information about this note. We can take the investigation in that direction if she seems suspicious."

It was still too early in the morning to call the author. Nikki and Harry took the ranger truck to get the four of us some coffee, leaving Antonio and me to continue working on the word puzzle.

"This is impossible," I said, dropping my pencil and leaning back in my chair.

"We have to keep trying," Antonio said. "It might be the key to finding the killer."

My eyes were starting to cross when an idea popped into my head. "Do you want to go out for lunch later today after we talk to the author?"

Antonio's face widened into a smile. "Are you asking me on a date, Rylie Cooper?"

"I guess I am," I said. "I mean, technically, we're not co-workers right now, right?"

He shrugged. "Even if we were, I would accept an offer to spend time with you."

His words both shocked and melted me at the same time.

"Great," I said. "Then it's a date."

Giddiness filled my chest. It was the first time I'd been on a first date since Garrett. And the fact that it was with Antonio was just icing on the cake.

"Did I just hear you ask Antonio on a date?" Nikki whispered in my ear, causing me to spin around, flailing.

My arms came into contact with the two travel cups she had in her hands. The lids popped off, and the coffee sprayed in the air like the steaming hot geysers at Yellowstone.

Nikki and I both screamed as the scalding liquid poured down on us.

"I'm so sorry," I said, pulling my shirt away from my chest so the coffee would cool.

"You should be," Nikki yelled as Antonio watched with widened eyes.

"You snuck up on me," I said. "What did you expect to happen?" I lowered my voice and hissed, "Especially with a murderer on the loose."

"You think a murderer would waltz into our park office and try to kill you?"

I sighed. "I'm sorry, okay? I shouldn't have karate chopped you when you whispered so creepily in my ear."

"Where's Harry?" I asked her, realizing he wasn't in the office.

"He had to go back to the station. He asked us to track down the author and see if she'd sit and talk to us."

"Can't he just pull up her address in his fancy police database?" I asked.

"He tried, couldn't find a record of her," Nikki said.

"Then I guess we're on our own," I said, glancing back at Antonio.

"I have to open the reservoir here in about a half hour, but I'll see you for lunch?"

I nodded. "See you then."

When we were back in the ranger truck, Nikki looked at me with raised eyebrows. "So?"

"So what?" I asked. "I already apologized. What else do you want from me? I'll buy you another coffee. Pay for your dry cleaning. Whatever." I leaned back against the seat and closed my eyes.

"I'm talking about Antonio," she said. "Are you guys a thing?"

"We're having lunch," I said. "It's not a big deal."

"But what about Luke?"

"I don't want to talk about Luke," I said.

I'd thought Luke and I were going to give it another shot. I thought he would end his contract in the Middle East and come home. Instead, he told me once again that he couldn't be my rebound and left on an airplane.

"Luke and I just aren't meant to be," I said. "We're better off as friends."

"And you think Antonio is your soulmate?"

"I don't know. Probably not," I admitted, "but I'm doing this thing I saw on that video app to revamp my life."

"Does it include you coming back to work? Because I think that alone would help revamp your life."

"This plan doesn't," I said, "but I am coming back."

Nikki nearly ran over a curb, taking a turn. "Really? Honestly? You're not just saying that to make me feel better?"

"Really. Being at the reservoir last night was enough to make me miss it."

"And seeing my beautiful face?" Nikki batted her long eyelashes.

"That too."

"Sorry about whatever happened with you and Luke. And about Shayla leaving. And about Garrett. I know it's been a rough couple of months."

"Garrett is engaged," I whispered.

"What?" Nikki practically yelled. "Who is he engaged to? It can't be Eloise. She's still in jail, right?"

"Not Eloise. I don't know who this woman is." I shrugged. "At least he didn't use the same ring."

"I have half a mind to go over there and shove my foot so far up his a—"

I interrupted her. "Okay, stop. Let's talk about something else."

"Fine," Nikki said, taking a deep breath. "How are we going to find the author's whereabouts?"

"Easy." I smiled. "Social media for the win." I pulled out my phone and navigated to the picture-scrolling app—a trick I'd gotten from Shayla during my recent trip. "Henrietta always posts where she wrote the day before. At coffee shops and such."

"But how does that help us today?" Nikki asked.

"Because she only goes to three different coffee shops

and all are in the Denver metro area. All we have to do is go to each of them until we find her."

Nikki glanced over as I scrolled through the pictures. "How do we know what she looks like? It doesn't look like she posts pictures of her face."

I pointed to the closed laptop in one of the flat-lay photos. "I'm guessing not everyone has a laptop cover with skulls and bloody daggers."

8

____

Besides the cozy atmosphere and the delicious chai latte, the first coffee shop was a bust.

By the time we reached the second coffee shop, it was nearly ten in the morning. If she wasn't at this one, we might have to wait until the next day to find her. Or message her and see if she'd meet us somewhere.

Thankfully, only two tables were occupied—one with a laptop and a skull and dagger cover. I glanced around to find who owned the computer—to get a peek at Henrietta Rose—but the only people in the room were the two baristas and a guy wearing gaming headphones in the corner.

"Let's order some coffee first," I said. "Maybe she's in the bathroom."

As we walked by the computer, the screen was open to what looked like pages of the novel that was set to be published this upcoming week. It took everything in me not to stop and read the words. I did catch the main character's name—Tiffany—on the page, though.

Nikki ordered for both of us—the same thing we had at the first coffee shop—while I watched the bathroom door.

Finally, as they handed our drinks over the bar, an unassuming woman with mousy brown hair and glasses walked out. I'd expected Henrietta to be older—in her fifties or sixties—but this woman wasn't much older than thirty, if that.

When she caught me staring, she pushed her glasses up on her nose and bent her head down, so her hair covered her face. She hurried over to the table and continued working.

"What are you waiting for?" Nikki asked. "Let's go talk to her."

I sucked in a breath and walked over with a smile. "Hi, Henrietta?"

The woman looked up at me.

"I'm Rylie Cooper," I said.

"I'm busy," she said in a quiet, squeaky voice.

"Right," I said. "Probably working on the next book, right? I'm a huge fan."

She looked me up and down as if she was skeptical of my claim on fandom.

"In fact, your books are the only books I read. I've never read writing as good as yours."

Her cheeks reddened as she pushed her glasses up on her nose again. "I'll be sure to pass that on. To the real Henrietta."

I glanced at Nikki.

"What do you mean, the real Henrietta?" I asked.

She giggled. "I'm Henrietta's personal assistant. I post

the pictures in the coffee shops. Henrietta doesn't leave her house."

"You pretend to be her?" Nikki asked. "Isn't that weird for you?"

The woman shrugged. "Many famous people have assistants who post to their social media profiles. Henrietta wouldn't be so loved if it weren't for all my pretending."

"We really need to speak with Henrietta," I said.

"She doesn't meet fans," the woman replied, closing the laptop and shoving it into her bag. "Sorry."

She was heading for the door when Nikki stepped in front of her. "I'm not a fan. We need to speak to her about a murder case. And we need to do it now. So either you can take us to her, or we can get an entire herd of police officers banging on her door and tromping through her house because you wouldn't let two polite young women speak to her."

The woman was physically shaking at Nikki's demand, but she didn't back down. "Can I see a badge?"

Nikki pulled out a badge I didn't recognize. It wasn't her ranger badge, but it wasn't a Prairie City PD badge, either.

Before I could get a good look, the woman relented. "Fine, I'll take you to her. But only the two of you. No one else."

Nikki nodded and followed her out the door, where she slid into a beautiful blue Audi E-Tron GT.

"That car is worth more than I'll make in five years," I said as Nikki and I hopped into the ranger truck.

"Apparently, being Henrietta Rose's assistant is a lucrative position."

"What was the deal with your badge back there?" I asked.

"I don't have the authority to talk to you about it," Nikki said. "Ursula would murder me."

"Kind of like you didn't have the authority to talk to me about these cases, yet you did anyway?"

Nikki stayed close to the blue sports car as the assistant wound down a street with relatively modest houses on either side.

"Oh, look," Nikki said. "I think we're here."

"But—"

"We can talk about it later," Nikki said, pulling into the driveway, which was a mere extension of the road. A brick house stood regally atop a slight hill as if presiding over all the other homes in the neighborhood.

When we got out of the truck, Nikki hurried up to the assistant. "I didn't catch your name."

"June," she said. "As in the month."

"And you said you've been working as Henrietta Rose's assistant for how long?"

"Only a couple of weeks. When her last assistant quit —she goes through them rather quickly—she pulled me into the position."

"This is a gorgeous house," I said as we approached the front steps where a security guard stood.

"This is only one of her properties," June said. "But she hardly leaves here anymore."

"Why wouldn't she sell the others?" Nikki asked. "Does she have kids or friends who use them?"

"No kids or spouse. The only things Henrietta cares about are her dogs and her typewriter." Irritation tinged June's voice. "You'll see in a second."

43

"No kids or spouse. The only things Henrietta cares about are her dogs and her typewriter." Irritation tinged June's voice. "You'll see in a second."

9

When the guard opened the door on June's orders, several tiny dogs came charging toward us, yapping their heads off.

"June? Is that you?" a gruff voice said from what sounded like a room down a hallway. "I thought I told you not to come back until you got that entire list done. Don't tell me you're finished already."

June sucked in a deep breath and closed her eyes. "There are some people here who want to talk to you."

A round of expletives I'd never heard in such an order came streaking down the hallway at us, followed by what sounded like a heavy barbell hitting a mat from a different room. When the sound died down, June said, "They're cops."

"You brought the cops into my house?" Henrietta shouted. "You're fired. You hear me? You're out of here. I've dealt with you for the last time. I don't care what you say. Enough is enough."

June turned to us and gave us a small smile. "It's

okay," she whispered. "She's not really firing me. Come on, let's get this over with."

As we walked through the foyer into the living room and then to a side room, we had to dodge various sculptures and pieces of furniture—careful not to knock over any of the tables holding tchotchkes.

When we made it through the door into the messiest office on the face of the planet, a robust woman in a long cream and flowered robe and matching hair wrap sat on one of those doctor-type stools at the desk, typing furiously on her typewriter.

"I told you, you're fired," Henrietta said without turning around. "Take your cop friends and get out."

"Henrietta, they just need your help assisting them with a murder investigation. As an expert."

"Ha! An expert," Henrietta shouted. "I thought you said I was a—"

"They're right here," June called over Henrietta. "Why don't you just talk to them?"

Henrietta swiveled around in her chair so quickly that her robe billowed out like a cape. Her face turned from anger to horror when she noticed Nikki and me. "Get out!" Henrietta yelled. "Get out now!"

"Ms. Rose," Nikki said. "We're with Prairie City Law Enforcement. We need to speak to you about a murder."

"Henrietta asked you to leave," a voice said behind us.

When I turned, I saw the person who presumably had been lifting weights—a tall, muscular woman in her mid-forties with coppery brown hair and the lightest blue eyes I'd ever seen.

"We only have a couple of questions," I said.

"They said if I didn't bring them, they'd have a bunch of police officers trampling through your house," June shouted.

"They'd have no such thing without a warrant to search this property or arresting me," Henrietta said. "Or do I have that wrong, too?"

June stared at Henrietta with wide eyes while the coppery brunette woman kept her gaze firmly planted on Nikki and me.

"Can we have five minutes?" I asked, my voice calm. "Just five. And if you want us to leave after that, we will."

Henrietta eased herself back onto the stool. "Five minutes. June, set a timer and come in when the five minutes are up. Uma, stay here in case you need to escort these women out."

June turned and walked out of the office, closing the door behind her. Uma—the coppery brunette—said nothing but stood with her arms crossed, watching us.

"Go ahead," Henrietta said. She was not at all what I was expecting. Honestly, it was slightly disappointing.

"I'll get straight to the point," I said. "There have been four murders and one attempted murder in the past few weeks that directly correlate with your Black is the New Dead Series."

"What do you mean they correlate with my series?" Henrietta asked.

"The murders have been set up exactly the way the murders happened in your books," I said. "Acid barrel, fake suicide, runner steps on a bomb, fire in a cabin, and a drowning."

Henrietta's eyes widened with every word I said.

"That's not possible," she finally said. "That makes no sense."

"It is possible," Nikki said. "And if Rylie hadn't read your books, we might not have known."

"Wasn't it on the news?" Henrietta asked.

"With all the politics, the news has bigger things to cover than a few dead bodies," Nikki said. "Plus, we've tried to keep the public details to a minimum so we could figure out what was going on."

I couldn't help but think if they had told the public about these murders, someone might have come forward sooner who recognized they were mimicking Henrietta's books.

"What is it you want from me?" Henrietta asked. "An apology? Mystery writers write about gruesome murders all the time. Mine aren't special. It isn't my fault some crazy person is trying to play out my ideas in real life."

"We want your help to figure out who has committed these murders," Nikki said. "Starting with the puzzle we found on the drowning victim."

"Right between the butt cheeks, just like you wrote," I said with a chuckle.

Henrietta didn't laugh. She didn't even smile. In fact, she looked like she'd just seen a ghost.

"I'm sorry, I can't help you. Your five minutes are over. Uma, please escort these women out."

I could not believe what I was hearing. This author—my favorite author—was turning down the chance to help with a murder investigation that stemmed from her books?

"Please, Henrietta," I said. "I love your books, and I

know you could be a very valuable asset to the investigation."

"I'm not a police officer," Henrietta said without turning back around. "I know who did it from the beginning. I don't have to figure it out. Good luck with your investigation."

Uma started toward Nikki and me. "Time to go."

June watched as we passed by her.

"I didn't expect Henrietta to be so . . . mean," I said.

Nikki didn't reply.

When we reached the front door, Uma said, "Get the hell out of here. You think Henrietta's mean? You should see me on a bad day."

Nikki and I hurried out of the office and back to her ranger truck.

"That was not at all how I thought that would go," I said as we sat in the driveway gathering our thoughts.

"Do you think she doesn't want to help because she committed the murders?" Nikki asked.

"I guess it's possible," I said, though I hated to admit it. "But she definitely doesn't fit the profile of the person we saw Antonio chasing last night."

"Something about her seemed off," Nikki said. "Like she knew more than she was saying. Plus, she's the one who created the murders. Maybe she's working with someone . . . like Uma or June. Did you see the picture of Henrietta and June from what looked like several years ago? There's history there."

"I guess it's possible," I said. "Though I'd bet money on Uma before I'd consider June."

"Who are the killers in the books?"

"Every book had a different killer. None of them were related to one another," I said. "And each of them goes to jail or dies at the end. It's very satisfying. You should read them."

"No time," Nikki said. "And, since we assume there's only one murderer, these are likely not the same as the books. Maybe she couldn't help us after all."

"How do we know there's only one murderer?" I asked. "Maybe there's some fan cult club who each took a book to reenact."

"Seems far-fetched," Nikki said. "But we could look into it."

I already had my phone out and was searching the Internet. "There are a few groups, but nothing that seems super cultish." I sighed.

"I know you don't want to think she's responsible, but is there any way she might do this for publicity? If this gets out to the press and is linked to her books, it could make people desperate to get their hands on the next one to see what happens."

She left out the part about seeing if someone might die similarly after the book was published. It was hard to argue the thought of this being a big, gruesome publicity stunt. Especially with the way Henrietta seemed to treat people.

A knock on my window made me jump in my seat.

June stood peeking in.

I rolled the window down.

"I have something I need to tell you."

June looked at the house behind her. "Not here. I need to discuss this with you away from her."

Nikki unlocked the doors. "Get in."

June hopped up into the back seat of the truck and slid down so anyone who might look out the window wouldn't see her. Nikki and I turned to the woman in the back. She looked like a child playing dress-up in her knee-length skirt, blouse, and heels.

"Well?" Nikki asked.

"You need to talk to her more," June said. "I think she did it."

I narrowed my eyes. "Hold on a second. Less than an hour ago, you were literally standing in the way of us talking to her. Now, you think she's responsible?"

"When you left, I heard her talking to her dogs about multiple murders based on her books."

"And . . ?" Nikki asked.

"If you'd have told me there were multiple murders that imitated her books, I would have instantly let you speak with her," June said. "If anyone can make something like that happen—with her own two hands or not—it's Bernie."

"Bernie?" I asked.

"I mean Henrietta," June quickly corrected.

"Why did you call her Bernie?" Nikki asked.

"It's a nickname," June said.

"You have a nickname for your boss?" Nikki asked.

June sat up slightly to peek out the window, then said, "This needs to stay between us."

Nikki and I exchanged glances, and both nodded. If it were pertinent to the case, it would most definitely not be kept between us.

"Henrietta Rose isn't her real name," June said. "It's a pseudonym. Her real name is Bernadette Herrigarta."

"Makes sense why she'd want to use a different name," Nikki said. "It also means she may have a record in the system under her true name. Can you spell the last name for me?"

June spelled it, and Nikki wrote it down in her notebook while I pulled out my phone and searched for her real name on the internet. The articles that popped up made me do a double-take. "Henrietta was a professional wrestler?" It didn't seem like she had the physique to be a wrestler. Though it looked like that was in her younger days.

"Henrietta's been about everything you can imagine," June said. "She was even a police officer for a while."

Which meant she knew the ins and outs of police work.

"She says it makes her books more realistic, but some

fans would disagree." June rolled her eyes. "Some people are never satisfied."

For how much she acted like she hated Henrietta, she also seemed weirdly protective of her. However, she was also the one accusing Henrietta of murder.

"What are those Band-Aids from?" I asked, noticing a couple of Band-Aids on her knee and legs. Maybe she was the person I'd chased through the field the night before.

"I had some cancerous spots removed," June said quietly. "I didn't think the Band-Aids were that noticeable."

"They're not super noticeable," I said.

She pulled one off, and it was evident the spot wasn't a fresh wound. "Maybe I don't need the Band-Aids anymore. A bit of coverup would probably be better."

"Where were you last night between the hours of nine and eleven?" Nikki asked, obviously not buying the cancer story, even though the wound beneath the Band-Aid was not fresh.

"Me?" June asked, picking at the wound. "I was on a date. I can get you his information and everything. And my doctor records about the spots. Anything to prove I didn't do this. You don't think I did this, do you?"

I looked over at Nikki. Did she?

"We just have to look into everyone who might know about the crimes," Nikki said. "Do you know where Henrietta was last night between the hours of nine and eleven?"

She seemed so formal with her questions.

"Probably on a walk with her dogs," June said. "She's

always walking her dogs when she's not in her office or sleeping. It's the only time she leaves the house."

"Could she have been in her office or sleeping?" I asked.

June shrugged. "Maybe. I wasn't here, but Uma might know."

I glanced back at the house. If I had to guess, Uma wouldn't be terribly forthcoming with information to help the case. But maybe one of the other security guards would be.

When the house door opened, I did not expect to see Henrietta storming toward our truck with her robe billowing out behind her and three of her tiny dogs running at her feet.

"Oh shit," June said. "She's gonna kill me."

"Get down on the floor and cover up with the blanket," Nikki said.

June got herself covered just in time for Henrietta to reach the truck.

"I thought I told the two of you to leave," Henrietta said. She looked much less old and frail in the daylight.

"We were just going over a couple of things here in the truck," Nikki said in a very calm voice. "We can move onto the street if you'd like us to."

Henrietta huffed and glanced around. "I didn't come out here to cause any more ruckus. I consulted with a colleague and decided it's my duty to help you in any way I can, seeing as how these murders are coming from the pages of my books."

I had to keep myself from asking if the colleague she

was speaking of was one of the ones currently yipping at her feet.

"That's great news, Ms. Rose," Nikki said.

"If we're going to be working together, you should probably know that my name is not actually Henrietta Rose. It's Bernadette Herrigarta. You can call me Bernie as long as we're not in front of any fans."

"Great," Nikki said. "Would you like to come with us, or shall we speak inside the house?"

"You're welcome to come back inside. I try not to leave when I don't have to." Bernie turned and walked back, her dogs following right along.

June waited until Nikki told her it was safe to come out.

When she popped up, she slipped out the other side of the truck and tiptoed back toward the house.

"This is weird," Nikki said.

"I'm not going in there until you tell me what's up with the badge." I crossed my arms over my chest.

Nikki closed her eyes and took a deep breath. "Ursula didn't want me to tell you this until you were officially back, but you are coming back, right? For sure?"

"Yes," I said. "For sure."

"Act surprised when she tells you about it, okay?"

"Just freaking tell me what the hell is going on."

"Ursula and Harry created a midpoint team at the beginning of the year. It's a new division for hybrid police slash park rangers. They made it for you . . . and then you didn't come back."

Anxiety welled in my chest. I hated letting people down. "If they'd told me—"

"They wanted you to want to come back, not feel obligated to come back because they created this team." Nikki put a hand on my arm. "You've made such a difference in Prairie City that they created a whole new division just so you—and other rangers and officers like you—could be exactly the type of officer you want to be."

My eyes welled up with tears. "I can't believe it."

"Believe it," Nikki said. "Now, enough of this. We have an author to talk to."

11

Walking back into Henrietta's—Bernie's—home a second time gave me a sensation I hadn't gotten the first. Maybe it was the way Uma followed us with a scowl on her face. Or perhaps it was that June thought her boss could be the killer.

Either way, this was no longer just my favorite author's home. This was a murder suspect's home.

"Come in, come in," Bernie said from the living room. She sat awkwardly on one of the overstuffed sofas while her dogs sat at her feet, looking up at her with the same look Fizzy gave me when he wanted to eat my dinner. Bernie, however, wasn't holding any food on her lap. "Please, sit down."

Nikki gestured to a picture on a table that looked like a younger version of Bernie and a high school-aged June in what might have been a cheerleading or school sports uniform. I didn't have time to examine it as we walked by.

"I'll get right into it," Nikki said when we sat on a

couch opposite Bernie. "Can you tell me where you were last night between nine and eleven o'clock?"

"I suppose I was walking my dogs," she said. "Or perhaps sleeping."

"You were sleeping," Uma said. "I walked the dogs last night."

"Oh, that's right." Bernie shifted in her seat and pulled her robe from beneath one of her legs.

"Do you have a security system, cameras, a phone, watch, or exercise tracker that may be able to corroborate this?" Nikki asked.

"I'm not much for technology—don't trust it," Bernie said, then looked at Uma.

"I don't have any such thing either," Uma said.

At this point, I realized Bernie didn't even have a TV.

Nikki looked like she was losing her patience. "Ms. Rose—Bernie—I am trying to help you here. At the moment, you are the most likely suspect for all these murders. But if you have an alibi for the times the murders took place, we might be able to keep you out of jail and could likely use your help to solve the crimes."

"Who better to help solve crimes than a mystery author?" I asked.

Nikki smirked at me, then turned her attention back to Bernie.

"I cannot believe you think I am responsible," Bernie said. "If word gets out that my books have anything to do with a string of murders in the area, my career will be over."

"Or it could be boosted," Nikki said. "It would likely get you nationwide attention."

"You can't possibly think I would kill people—that anyone would kill people—for publicity."

"People kill people for publicity all the time."

"Not authors," Bernie said. "Name one author who actually killed someone."

"Wasn't an author just arrested because she killed her husband after writing a book about how to get away with killing your husband?" I asked.

Nikki and Bernie both gaped at me.

I shrugged. "I turned off the normal news. Now, I get a lot of book news." It was surprising Bernie hadn't at least heard about it.

"Let's go back to that alibi," Nikki said.

"Last night," Bernie scrunched up her nose. "Last night, I was outlining the seventh book in the series. I got through chapter eight and called it for the night. My babies were begging for a walk, but I was too tired." She reached down and scratched the pups at her feet behind their ears. "Uma took all five of them together while I went to bed."

Nikki was writing notes as I sat there like an idiot without a notepad or a pen.

I turned to Uma. "Did you see anyone on the walk who could corroborate your being with the dogs last night?"

"Now you think Uma did this?" Bernie asked with a look of horror on her face.

"We have to explore all the possibilities," I said.

"How about a week ago, Tuesday?" Nikki said. "Do you know where you were between noon and midnight?"

"That's a huge time frame." Bernie stood. "Let me go check my calendar."

She hurried into her office and started shuffling papers around like her life depended on it. Uma positioned herself between us and Bernie's office doorway.

"Do you really think Bernie could have done it?" I whispered to Nikki so Uma couldn't hear.

Nikki shook her head slightly. "I don't know, but we have to get their alibis. It's part of the procedure."

When a crash came from the office, Nikki and I rushed in to find Bernie on her back with her five dogs licking her face and a short bookshelf on top of her. Tchotchkes were broken all around her.

Tears streamed down Bernie's plump cheeks as Uma pulled the bookshelf off her like it was nothing, then helped her to a stand.

"I can't find it," Bernie said. "My calendar is gone."

12

Taking in the contents of the office, it was no surprise Bernie couldn't find her calendar. Papers with typewritten lines and paragraphs and lists littered every surface. Books—both Bernie's own and those of others—were turned upside down with tabs and miscellaneous bookmarks sticking out.

"Where were you trying to find it when the shelf fell on you?" I asked.

"I wanted to see if it fell behind there." Bernie plopped down on her doctor-type stool. Its pneumatic height adjustment compensated by lowering her slightly to the ground. "It shouldn't have, but when it wasn't on my desk, I didn't know where else to look. Someone had to have taken it."

I glanced at Nikki, who looked just as suspicious of that theory as I was.

"Why don't we help you clean up your office," I said, reaching down to pick up the pieces of the broken figurines. "Maybe we'll find it then."

Nikki grabbed a handful of papers.

"NO!" Bernie let out a scream so loud the dogs began howling like fluffy little monsters.

Nikki dropped the papers and backed away. "I'm sorry. I didn't know."

Bernie did her best to put the papers back where they'd been. "It might look like a mess to you, but everything is exactly where I need it—exactly where I'll be able to find it."

"Except your calendar," Nikki said.

"Which is why I think someone took it." Bernie glared at her with a huff.

"And who do you think could have taken it?" Nikki asked.

"Do you want a list?" Bernie's demeanor was a challenge, and Nikki wasn't backing down.

"Go for it." Nikki pulled out her pen and paper.

I shifted my weight from one foot to the other, staring down at the broken giraffe in my hands.

"My ex-husband, to start," Bernie said. "He was here just the other day demanding I give him more money in alimony since my new series has done so well the past few months. I told him to take it up with the judge. Of course, he can't afford a lawyer because he spends all his money on his new plaything."

I didn't know what was stranger—that Bernie had been married or that she'd let her ex into her office.

"In fact, I bet he took my calendar so he could frame me for the murders he committed," Bernie said.

Nikki stopped writing and glanced up at her. "Hold on. You think he murdered these people?"

"I can't think of anyone else as vindictive as he is," Bernie said. "Unless you count my old assistants, but I don't know that any of them are smart enough to pull off a murder."

"Can you give us your ex-husband's name, phone number, and residential address?" Nikki asked.

"Happy to," Bernie said. "His name is Percy Baker." She rattled off his telephone number and address. "But he likely won't be home until the wee hours of the morning. He owns a strip club over near the military base."

"How does a guy who owns a strip club need money?" I asked.

"He pisses it all away somehow," Bernie said. "Don't ask me. That's why I fired him."

"You mean divorced," Nikki corrected.

"Basically, the same thing." Bernie shrugged. "Is there anything else I can help you with?"

"Can we look around?" Nikki asked.

Bernie shook her head. "Not unless you have a warrant."

I pulled up the picture of the butt crack puzzle on my phone. "Can you decipher this? It's just like the one in your book."

She yanked my phone from my hand. "Let me see."

We watched as she studied the photo. She wheeled her stool over to her desk with the typewriter and started free-hand writing on a sheet of paper next to it.

Nikki glanced at me, and I shrugged. Hopefully, she figured it out, and it would point us to the killer.

After what seemed like ages, Bernie turned around and

handed me my phone. "Sorry, I don't know." Her voice shook when she spoke.

Nikki and I gaped at her.

"But then, what's all that?" I asked, peeking around her at the paper she'd been writing on.

She snatched it out of my line of sight, crumpled it into a ball, and put it down her shirt. "It's nothing."

"Bernie, if you know something based on that note, it could really help the case," I said. "Don't you want to find out who did this?"

"I couldn't make out what the note says," Bernie said, her tone increasingly panicked. "I can't help you."

With that, she stood from her stool. "You need to leave now. Uma, get them out of here."

Nikki and I turned and walked out of her office before Uma could physically remove us.

"If you're withholding evidence from the authorities, that's a crime," I yelled behind me. "You're hindering our investigation."

"I'm doing no such thing," Bernie yelled back. "I couldn't decipher the note. That's all there is to it. Talk to Percy. I'd bet my left eye he has something to do with it. And while you're there, tell him he's not getting another cent from me."

Uma slammed the door behind us, and the sound of a lock clicking into place was the perfect representation of my thoughts on the case. We'd hit a dead end.

13

When we pulled out of Bernie's driveway, my stomach rumbled, reminding me I had a lunch date.

"We need to get this information over to Harry and see where we should go from here," Nikki said. "I'm all for going to the strip club to question this guy if that's what needs to happen."

"Me too," I said. "But, uh, could you drop me at my house, and you can talk to Harry alone?"

"Right, you have a date with Antonio," Nikki said, her voice teasing. "I forgot."

"I don't think it's an actual date," I said. "He's not usually into girls like me."

Nikki let out a hissing sound. "You're right. He's not into girls *like* you. He's into you."

"You don't know that," I said. "He's been dating a lot."

"Not seriously," Nikki said. "I think he's secretly waiting for his chance to date you."

Queasiness took over my stomach. Whether it was a

good queasiness or a bad queasiness was still undetermined. "It's just lunch," I said, trying to keep my expectations in check.

"Keep telling yourself that," Nikki said. "But, yes, I'll drop you at your house, and I'll go talk to Harry. If you're truly coming back, we need to get you a uniform and badge, and Ursula will have to sign your papers for the training program."

"Training program?"

"Don't worry about it," Nikki said. "It's not a huge deal. You'll breeze right through it."

"And we don't have to carry guns, right?"

Nikki shook her head. "We can if we want to, but that takes a whole other certification."

"I don't think I will."

"I definitely will."

"About the case," I said. "Do you think the ex-husband could really be responsible? It seems pretty far-fetched."

"I still think Bernie and possibly Uma are our best suspects," Nikki said. "Uma seemed strong enough to get a barrel full of acid into the water. And since Bernie was a police officer, she knows all the ins and outs of investigations. Even though she commented how this would hurt her career, there's no chance it would. The minute the news latches onto these cases, people will scramble to read her books—especially the newest one. We live in a society of armchair detectives and true crime nuts."

She was right. This would only boost Bernie's sales. "Maybe the ex-husband did it to boost her sales so he'd get more alimony."

Nikki tilted her head. "That's a thought."

We pulled up to my apartment building, and I got out of the truck.

"Keep your phone on so you can hear if I call you," Nikki said. She knew I always kept it on either silent or vibrate mode. Hardly anyone called me anyway. "After you're done with Antonio, go talk to Ursula. Make sure she pays you for your time these past two days."

When I'd first met Nikki, I never would have thought she'd end up mother-henning me. "I will. See you later."

She pulled away, and I hurried up to my apartment to change and freshen up. I'd been in the same clothes for over twenty-four hours, and my t-shirt under my hoodie was covered in dried coffee.

Fizzy ran circles around my legs when I walked in. "Don't act like you've been here all alone. I know Mom came over and fed and walked you."

He lowered his chest to the floor and wagged his tail in a playful pose.

"I'll be home later, and we can play," I said. "Right now, I have to get ready for a date."

I changed as quickly as possible before throwing my hair into a ponytail and swiping on some mascara. "That'll have to do." I hugged and kissed Fizzy on the way back out. "I love you. Be a good boy."

Antonio hurried to open the restaurant door when I arrived. "I thought perhaps you changed your mind."

"Nikki and I got held up in an interview with the

author. Then, I had to run home and change, so I looked semi-human."

Antonio did a quick once-over of my outfit. "You look more than semi-human. You look stunning."

He was coming on strong already. I couldn't help but blush. He'd always had a way of making me feel both dangerous and safe at the same time.

"You don't look too bad yourself," I said with what I hoped was a natural smile. He looked more than not too bad. He looked amazing. And smelled amazing. His jeans and black t-shirt fit his muscular body as if they were made specifically for him. The leather jacket he always wore hung over a chair at a table by the window.

"I hope you don't mind. I already sat at the table," he said. "But I have not ordered anything. I wanted to wait for you."

"I don't mind at all," I said. "I'm the one who was late."

He led me to the table, pulled my chair out, then sat across from me.

"This is a great view." Out the window was a small tree-lined park with a pond filled with geese.

Antonio shrugged. "This is one of my favorite places— it is kind of a hole in the wall but has fantastic food and service."

I thought of the first time Luke and I had enjoyed a meal together after I'd become a Prairie City ranger. Every waitress in the place knew him by name and flirted like their lives depended on it.

Not here, though. Our server was an incredibly profes- sional man. I shook my head. I didn't need to go down the rabbit hole of comparing Luke and Antonio. One was here. The other wasn't. That's all that mattered.

"What do you recommend?" I asked after the waiter took our drink orders. "Everything sounds so good."

"I usually get the calamari to begin, then move onto the ziti. It's almost as good as my mother's."

I closed my menu. "Sold. I'll do the same, though, maybe we can just share a plate of calamari?"

Antonio nodded, and when the waiter returned with our drinks, he ordered for both of us while glancing at me to ensure that was what I still wanted.

"How is the investigation?" Antonio asked, leaning back in his chair and draping his arm over the back. With his other hand, he brought his water to his full, delicious lips. "Rylie?"

When the glass missed the table, I nearly dropped my water, but my reflexes corrected just in time. "The investigation? It's fine. We got nowhere. The author's alibis are flimsy at best. She said it was probably her ex-husband trying to ruin her life. Or maybe boost her sales so he can benefit from an increased alimony payment." I shook my head. "So basically nowhere."

"What about the note? Could she figure it out?"

"She worked on it for a few minutes—more than a few, several minutes—before telling Nikki and me she couldn't solve it. When I asked to see the notes she'd taken, she wadded them up and shoved them down her shirt."

Antonio burst out laughing. He didn't laugh very often, but it was a delightful sound when he did. It made me want to make him laugh over and over again.

Shayla would be so mad when I told her I'd gone on a

date with Antonio. She was a Luke fan to the core—probably because before getting engaged to the love of her life, she'd had a thing for Luke.

When Antonio finally regained his composure, he stared at me over the newly delivered calamari. "You're hilarious."

"*I* didn't shove it down my shirt," I said. "But it is slightly funny that the possible answer to the butt crack code went between her boobs."

This sent Antonio into another fit of laughter, and this time, I couldn't help but laugh along with him.

14

With full stomachs and aching cheeks from all the laughter we'd shared, Antonio and I walked out of the restaurant almost—but not quite—touching.

"This was really fun," I said as we approached Cherry Anne.

"We should do it again sometime . . . soon," Antonio said, reaching down and interlocking his fingers with mine.

A chill ran up my arm and sent my neck hairs on end. "What about being co-workers?"

"I am assuming Nikki already spoke with you about the hybrid division. If you decide to join, we wouldn't technically be co-workers anymore. At least not in the hierarchy of things. You would be a completely separate entity."

He made a good point. People from different divisions could date per city employment rules.

Before I could say anything, a strange sound came from somewhere near me.

I let go of Antonio's hand to figure out what it was.

Was it coming from my purse? Had someone put an electronic key tag in there to track me? I was always so careful looking for ways human traffickers tagged cars, but I never thought they'd manage to get something in my purse.

I dug through the contents, furiously looking for the little tag.

"Are you okay?" Antonio asked a look of amusement on his face.

"I think someone's put a tracking key tag in my purse." The sound went off again, louder, with my purse open.

"Uh, yes, if you call your phone a tracking key tag," Antonio said.

I shook my head. "My phone doesn't make that noise."

"Did you recently join a new dating app?"

My face flamed with realization. This was probably the notification sound for Just Personalities, meaning I had matches. Or dates. Or whatever the app called them.

"How did you—wait—are you on Just Personalities too?"

Antonio shrugged. "I am on all the apps. You never know where you will find the love of your life." He looked down at his shoes as if he wanted to say more but didn't.

"Looks like I have my first matches," I said.

"Be careful with that app. Since you don't get to see what the people look like, you can get some pretty outrageous matches. Not that I don't like women with spiked blood-red hair or ones with big hairy moles on their knees, but that's just the way the app works, I guess."

I laughed at the thought of the spiked blood-red hair. I bet that had been a shock.

I turned my phone screen off and pushed it back into my purse. "I don't think I need the app at this point." I reached down and grabbed his hand again.

A look of shock and maybe fear washed over Antonio's face. I'd never seen him so unsure about anything.

"Do you remember Christmas Eve a couple of years ago?"

"The night you kissed me?" Antonio asked.

"I believe you kissed me," I corrected.

"I think about it all the time," Antonio said. "I wish I had told you how I felt before you got engaged and almost married."

Almost was the keyword in that sentence. "But I didn't get married."

"God gave me a second chance with you," Antonio said. He reached his fingers up to my neck and leaned in.

He was going to kiss me.

My lips parted in a smile. Then I closed them so he wouldn't kiss my teeth

But what if my lips felt rigid?

I tried to let them stay loose. But not too loose. Just the right amount of loose.

Antonio was pulling away before I'd even realized we'd kissed.

"Is everything okay?" Antonio asked. "You seem tense. I am very sorry if you did not want me to kiss you. I didn't mean to push things too fast."

I wanted to stop his rambling, but my mouth was now so rigid it couldn't form words.

"Oh, Rylie," Antonio said. "Please forgive me. I did not mean to take things too far. It's just our kiss on Christmas Eve was magical. I have been longing to kiss you again since that night."

I'd thought of that kiss more than any engaged woman should have. So why couldn't I tell him?

As I tried to form the words—any words—my phone made that sound in my purse again. The one that notified me I had another match.

Antonio looked at my purse, defeated. "You can check those. Maybe it is for the best that we just stay friends."

He opened my car door for me, and I slipped inside.

"Thank you for lunch," I squeaked out.

He smiled. "Anytime."

As he walked away, I felt the urge to run after him, but what felt like a weight in my chest held me back. I couldn't get into a relationship right now. Luke was right. I wasn't ready. Antonio was great, but I wasn't ready. I couldn't even remember how to kiss someone.

This list was stupid.

I pulled out my phone, ignored the notification for the match—that was the last thing I needed—and opened the video app. I went straight to the video with the list of things to do and added a comment.

This list is not working. Things have just gotten worse.

I hit send. Before closing the app, I had a notification that said the video's creator had responded to my comment. Great, she would probably tell me off for bashing her program. Usually, I only commented positively. What had gotten into me? I didn't need the confrontation right now.

I tapped the button for the notification to take me to her reply.

> *Let me guess. You're on day two*

My heart raced in my chest.

How did you know that?

> *Day two is the hardest. Going out on a date or out with friends when you've been secluded for so long can be exhausting. Keep going. I promise it'll get better*

I didn't know how to reply.

Thanks.

I closed the app and put my phone back in my purse. Keep going. Which meant moving onto day three—getting a new pet.

15

On my way home, I got a text from Nikki.

When you're finished with your date, go home and get some sleep. We're going to the strip club at midnight.

After walking Fizzy, I settled into my bed for a nap but couldn't fall asleep. My thoughts kept going back to how Antonio was feeling and how I'd messed everything up with him. I'd written and deleted at least a dozen text messages, but nothing quite said how I felt.

I needed something else to focus on, so I went to the last book Bernie had written. Maybe if I looked through it, I could figure out the cipher myself. It hadn't seemed that hard for the sleuth once she knew what she was looking for.

MBIP'Q AV I VIWE?

I searched the internet for clues about how to solve the puzzle, but I just didn't have a lot to work with. Bernie had obviously figured it out but hadn't wanted to share the results.

The more I tried to solve it, the more confused I became. My vision blurred, and the next thing I knew, my alarm was blaring in my ear.

I stood and stretched so I wouldn't hit the snooze button and be late for meeting Nikki.

My brain returned to the code, but even after sleep, I wasn't seeing anything new.

If only Bernie would have been upfront with us. It was apparent she knew what the code meant.

I pulled up to the strip club expecting—well—a club-type atmosphere outside with bouncers and a line and fancy cars.

There was none of that.

In fact, the only way I knew it was a strip club was because of the sign in the dirty window of the old brick building.

"This is the club Bernie's husband owns?" I asked Nikki when we got out of our cars. She drove a BMW that her father had likely bought her. Not that I could complain, since my car had been gifted to me.

"Makes more sense now why he'd need money from her," Nikki said, leading the way inside. She wore a pair of black pleather pants, incredibly high pink heels, and a matching top. Her hair was teased within an inch of its life on top of her head.

I glanced down at my jeans and heels combination and silently wished I'd done a better job getting ready. I didn't look anywhere near as good as she did.

The interior of the building was slightly better than the exterior. The smell of stale smoke permeated the air even though smoking wasn't allowed inside the building anymore and probably hadn't been for years.

Black carpet led to black walls and a black stage in the center of a room with shiny stripper poles and five or six naked—besides their heels—women dancing on them. I averted my eyes, but not before I noticed the quality of the strippers didn't seem to be terribly high.

Though the quality of the patrons wasn't terribly high, either.

Nikki walked over to the bar as if there weren't naked women shaking their lady bits all over the place and asked the bartender to speak with Percy.

"What the hell are you looking at?" The giant of a man beside Nikki gave her a dirty look before moving a couple of stools down.

The bartender gave each of us a once over, and his face widened into a grin. "Are you here to audition?"

"That's for Percy to know," Nikki said, batting her long eyelashes.

He scurried off to get his boss while Nikki did a glance around the place.

"It's definitely not your cream of the crop strip club," she said, just as one of the women fell completely off the pole onto her butt.

"These guys like the subpar dancers," a man's voice

said, coming up behind us. "It makes them think they have a shot with them. If they were supermodels, we'd lose half our clientele because they'd feel too intimidated."

"I'm guessing you're Percy," Nikki said to the man, who was only about five foot five, with a black comb-over and cowboy boots.

"And by the looks of you, you're not strippers. At least you're not," he said to Nikki, then turned to me. "You could be, but not here. You're too pretty for a place like this. You could probably work at one of those high-class strip joints."

I didn't know whether to be offended or flattered.

"I have a professional eye that can spot a stripper from a mile away. Even future strippers. They just have a sort of aura about them." He seemed incredibly proud of this strange skill.

"Interesting," I said.

"Can we go somewhere a bit quieter to talk?" Nikki asked, nearly shouting over the bass of the music.

"Depends on what you want to talk about," Percy said.

"We're here about a couple of murders—"

Percy interrupted her. "Nope. I don't talk to cops. I didn't murder anyone. You can speak to my lawyer."

He turned to walk away, but Nikki cut him off. "It has to do with your ex-wife."

"Did she finally kill someone for real?" He glanced behind us at the bartender, who was pouring another drink for the guy who hadn't wanted to sit next to Nikki.

"That's what we're trying to figure out," Nikki said.

"If I had to bet, I'd say it was her. But I'm not a betting

man, and you're not welcome here." He pushed past us and stormed out of the room through a doorway in the back.

"That went well," I said. "Looks like we won't get much out of him."

Nikki shook her head. "But maybe we could get something out of his girls."

"My guess is we won't get anywhere with them until their shift is over at two," I said. "We can wait in here or out in the car."

"I vote car," Nikki said.

"Agreed."

We sat in her BMW because even though Cherry Anne was a new model, her car was nicer.

"Have you told Ursula yet?" Nikki asked.

I slapped my forehead. "I forgot. Do you think I should send her a message now?"

Nikki shook her head. "She keeps her phone on at all times. You'll just wake her."

I put a reminder in for nine tomorrow morning. "I'm excited to come back."

"We're excited to have you back."

"You seem to be doing just fine without me," I said, slightly irritated with myself for the blatant request for validation.

"Are you serious?" Nikki laughed. "We have five unsolved murders on our hands. That all started right after we created the hybrid division. Why they couldn't have killed people somewhere other than in Prairie City parks is beyond me."

"Oh, that makes sense. We only look into crimes committed in the parks," I said.

Nikki looked at me like I was a complete dumbass. "Yeah."

"Sorry, I've been a bit off my game lately."

"Well, get on your game. We need to solve these murders quickly before the next book comes out and we have another victim."

"Maybe we can get the book before it's released to the public so we can be prepared."

"Or maybe we can talk Bernie out of publishing it," Nikki said. "If she doesn't publish the book, the murderer won't know who to kill next."

I considered this. It was a solid plan. Unless Bernie was the killer.

16

Nikki opened the oversized center console in her BMW to reveal a fully stocked pantry. "Need a snack?"

I was always up for a snack. I chose a Reese's double pack and a bag of Doritos.

"Healthy as always," Nikki said, closing it after getting nothing for herself. "How did things go with Antonio?"

"Not good," I said. "He kissed me and I wasn't ready and there was zero spark. I didn't even know the kiss happened until it was over and he was apologizing and I couldn't form any words, so I basically got in my car and sped away."

Nikki gaped at me.

"Okay, so it wasn't that bad, but it was pretty bad." I shoved an entire peanut butter cup into my mouth.

"Do you like him?"

"Yesh," I said, my mouth still full of chocolate peanut buttery goodness.

"Gah, don't talk with your mouth full," Nikki said. "It's disgusting."

I finished chewing the treat with my mouth wide open just to gross her out.

"Mature, real mature," Nikki said, but she was smiling, so I knew she wasn't too mad about it.

When I'd swallowed, I said, "Yes, I like him. In fact, I considered leaving Garrett for him at one point."

"What? When?" Nikki asked. "What about Luke?"

"You and Luke were dating," I said. It was a bit of a sore subject. When she and Luke dated, apparently, Luke talked about me a lot. But it had been his decision then, just like now, not to be my rebound. Ugh.

"Then what's the problem? If you like him, why not go for it?"

"Because the stupid voice in my head is telling me it's too soon, and I need to recover from my breakup first."

"Valid," Nikki said. "Only you'll know when you're ready."

"How are you and Naked—uh—Oliver?"

Nikki sighed. "We're great. He's taking me to Mexico this summer."

"Is he going to run naked down the beach there?" I couldn't help myself. She'd started dating the guy who was notorious for running naked through our parks. He'd been arrested and kicked out more times than I could count.

"We both are," she said. "It's a nude resort."

I could feel my jaw drop open. Thankfully, I'd just swallowed most of the chip I'd shoved into my mouth moments before, or Nikki probably would have kicked me out of her car. "You're going to a nude resort."

"Oh my gosh, Rylie. You're such a prude. It's just flesh. And it's freeing." She tossed her hair over her shoulder. "I saw how you looked at those women in there—like they're beneath you. Well, they're not. And if you don't treat them respectfully, they'll probably not answer any of our questions."

"Wanna bet?" I asked. I had no intention of disrespecting them, but I wanted to prove to Nikki that I could get them to talk just as well as she could.

"How much?"

"Five hundred."

"Dollars?" Nikki asked. "Do you even have that much money?"

I shrugged. "I guess you'll find out."

She pulled five one-hundred-dollar bills from her wallet and nodded. "You have yourself a deal."

Now I just needed a plan.

When the neon open sign finally went dim, Nikki and I sat perched on the edge of our seats, waiting for the women to walk outside.

The plan I'd come up with in my head was far from fleshed out—no pun intended—but it would have to do. Otherwise, I'd be handing over the last of my savings to a woman who could use hundred-dollar bills as toilet paper.

"Do you think they'll have bodyguards who come out with them?" I asked.

"There weren't even bouncers at the entrance," Nikki noted. "I'd say it's likely they're on their own."

I counted the number of cars in the parking lot—twelve. Even if everyone who worked in the club had their own cars, that still left a few unaccounted for. Which meant my plan might just work.

"Here they come," Nikki said.

Four of the women walked out in a group, huddled together, as two men followed closely behind.

Nikki and I stepped out of the car and approached.

"Do you want to try first?" Nikki asked.

I shook my head. "Be my guest."

Nikki approached, and the two men stopped her. "That's close enough."

"What are you, their bodyguards?"

"No," the shorter of the two men said, "we're their dates."

Just as I'd suspected.

"Their dates?" Nikki asked.

"Yep, they're going out with us tonight," the other man said.

When Nikki looked at the women, they just smiled and shrugged.

"How about they do that another night?" Nikki said. "My friend and I need to have a chat with them."

I glanced around. We needed to do this before Percy came out and put a kibosh on everything.

"We're okay," one of the women said, "but thanks."

Nikki glanced at me. I guess that meant it was my turn.

"How much are they paying you to spend the night with them?" I asked.

The women looked at each other and then at the guys.

The same woman said, "Fifty bucks each."

"Fifty bucks?" I asked, shaking my head. "That's it?"

"Hey, that's enough," the taller guy said. "They agreed. It's not like we're forcing them."

"How about I pay you each a hundred bucks to spend an hour chatting with us?" I said. "And I'll throw in snacks."

I didn't have the guts to look at Nikki, but I could feel the tension growing in her body as she realized what I was up to.

The women exchanged a quick look and then nodded. "Yeah, that's a better deal. Sorry guys, maybe another time."

"Oh, come on, you already took all our money in the club," the shorter one said with an annoying whine in his voice. "You practically owe us."

Nikki stepped between the men and the women. "They owe you nothing. Get in your cars and leave."

"Whoa, jeez," the taller guy said. "It's all good. We'll keep our money and catch up with you ladies tomorrow night."

17

The women smiled and waved as the men walked away. When the men drove out of the parking lot, their demeanors changed.

"Holy shit, thank you," the woman wearing a leopard print miniskirt said. "Those guys are creeps."

"Why would you agree to go with them, then?" I asked. "You know what they wanted, right?"

"Yeah, we know," the woman with big green false eyelashes that matched her heels said. "They pay us at least once a week to go with them. Sometimes they get what they want, but they pass out before anything happens most of the time, and we're fifty dollars richer."

"Which reminds me." I turned to Nikki. "Pay up."

"Oh no, you don't even have to pay us," the woman in the miniskirt said, and the others nodded. "Honestly, it's just nice we got off the hook tonight."

Nikki raised an eyebrow at me. There was absolutely no way I would let her off the hook for this bet. She wouldn't have let me off the hook, even though she knew how poor I was.

"Come on, Nikki, what are you waiting for? A deal's a deal."

"Am I a bet?" The shortest of the women said in a horrendously shrill voice. "Am I a dumbass bet?"

"It's stupid, not dumbass. If you're gonna quote a movie, get it right," the green-eyelashed woman said, and they all burst out laughing.

As Nikki doled out the cash, I said, "We bet on which one of us could get you guys to talk to us first. And I just happened to win."

"And you bet five hundred dollars?" Miniskirt asked.

"I didn't know how many of you I'd be dealing with," I said, handing each of them a hundred-dollar bill which they stashed in various places on their bodies. "And this way, I get to keep a hundred for myself."

"What about the snacks?" the tiny one asked. "You said there'd be snacks."

"Come on over to Nikki's car," I said. "She has a whole center console cupboard full of snacks."

Nikki's eyes widened as she looked from me to the women and back again. "But—I—"

"What? You don't want these fine, upstanding women in your car?"

They gasped, and the tiny one looked like she might cry.

"No," Nikki said, actually showing a shred of kindness. "I mean, yes. Of course, you can come in my car. But the back seat is only big enough for three people and—"

"We gotta go," I said, pointing at the entrance where Percy, the bartender, and the giant guy from the bar were coming out. Percy yelled at the guy from the bar, "You're not welcome here. Stay away from her." The bartender pushed the enormous man away from them, though the man didn't seem to feel the push at all. He held his hands up in surrender and hurried to a small silver car that looked like a rental.

Nikki and I each grabbed two of the women and pulled them to her car while the women tried to keep up in their massive heels.

I flung open Nikki's door and shoved my two in while she did the same on the other side.

"Do you think they saw us?" I asked Nikki, trying to crane my neck to get a glimpse of Percy, only to find four terrified women in the back seat.

"You can have your money back," Miniskirt said, holding out her hundred-dollar bill. "I don't want anything to do with whatever you're doing."

The other three held out their hundred-dollar bills, too.

"I'm sorry, that was abrupt," I said. "We're not doing anything illegal. In fact, we're with law enforcement."

"Law enforcement?"

Their eyes widened as they all screamed, dropped the money, and flew out of the car like it was on fire.

As the doors slammed shut, Nikki looked at me with a glare.

"What?" I asked. "They would have found out when we started asking them about the murders."

"They were illegally prostituting themselves, and you told them we're cops."

"I said we're in law enforcement."

"Same thing," Nikki said. "No one who hears the words law enforcement thinks about park rangers."

She had a point.

"Looks like I get my money back."

I fished the hundred-dollar bill out of my jeans pocket while Nikki picked up the other four bills from the back seat floor.

"Now, who are we going to talk to?" I asked.

Nikki glanced out the windshield as the women sprinted, not to their cars but to Percy.

Percy's eyes narrowed at us when the women pointed to Nikki's car.

"Get in your car," Nikki said. "We gotta go."

I jumped out of her car and into mine.

She hit the accelerator and tore out of the parking lot.

I pushed the button to start the car, but nothing happened. I pushed it again and again, but the car didn't even try to start. It was then I realized I'd left my purse in Nikki's car along with my proximity key fob and my phone.

I locked the doors just as Percy was reaching for the handle.

"What are you doing harassing my girls?" Percy screamed. "I told you to talk to my lawyer."

I yelled back so he could hear me through the window. "I just wanted to ask if they knew your whereabouts when the murders occurred."

This got his attention. "You think I killed people?"

"You are overly defensive, told us to contact your lawyers before you even knew what we had to say, and are trying to break into my car right now," I said. "That makes me think it's a definite possibility."

"Ridiculous," he shouted. "I didn't kill anyone. I'll give you alibis up the wazoo. Bernie told you it was me, didn't she? I bet she didn't tell you about all the assistants she's fired in the past year. I mean, not the most recent one she fired—that's my fiancée—but the other ones. Maybe one of them did it to ruin her career."

Was I the only one who had heard the saying—bad publicity is still publicity?

"I think you did it to boost her career so you could get more money out of her," I said.

"Why would I need more money?" he shouted. "I make bank here. Did Bernie tell you I was begging for money when I went over there? Because I wasn't. I know I broke the restraining order, but I had to talk to her. She tells everyone I'm begging for money to make me look like a piece of shit. Just because I fell in love with someone else. Well, it wasn't hard when I wasn't ever in love with her in the first place. And it's not my fault she hired such a beautiful assistant. She should have kept to the ugly ones."

My head spun with all the information in that statement.

"Have the *real* police talk to me about a statement," he said before I could reply. "And get off my property."

18

I tried to yell after Percy that I couldn't get off his property because I didn't have my keys, but he either didn't hear me or didn't care. He strutted back over to the group of women and tried to hug them with his short arms. They ducked down to accommodate him.

I sighed and wondered how long it would take Nikki to realize she had my purse. If only I hadn't turned the ringer off when I threw it in my purse as I headed out my apartment door. I couldn't stand the sound of the notifications for that Just Personalities dating app.

Thankfully, Percy, the bartender, and the women all got into their cars and left without another glance my way.

I laid my head back and closed my eyes. What a crazy night.

I replayed what Percy had said before storming away. He didn't need money, so he might not have been at Bernie's house recently. That could have been a lie. He'd also fallen in love with one of her assistants, presumably before Bernie fired her and filed for divorce, effectively firing him from her life too.

I must have fallen asleep as I mulled the details over in my head. My eyelids flew open at the violent jolting of my car.

I sat up and glanced out the windshield to find I was being towed.

Didn't they even look inside a car before they hooked it up and drove away?

How long had I been sleeping? The sun was up, and Nikki was nowhere around. Surely, she'd seen my purse by now and knew where I was.

But if that were the case, I'd be driving home, not being towed to an impound lot.

I put my seatbelt on for good measure and waited out the bumpy ride. Everything would be fine if the tow truck driver kept driving like they were.

Too bad the driver took the interstate, where traffic moved at either a snail's pace or lightning speed. At this time of day, it was the speed of lightning, and this driver seemed to think he was in the race of his life.

I held onto the door and the steering wheel, bracing myself for impact.

I always heard bracing yourself was the worst thing you could do, but I was so terrified I couldn't help it.

Finally, he took an exit and drove straight into the gates of what seemed to be a police impound lot. However, it wouldn't have been a Prairie City lot because we weren't even close to Prairie City. Which meant if this were a police impound lot, I wouldn't know any of the officers. And I didn't have a fancy badge like Nikki.

But they'd have a phone.

Except I didn't know any phone numbers, but my parents' and my sister's by heart.

I sighed. I'd call my sister first, but she was unlikely to answer in the middle of the day. It was her personal time, and she literally shut off her phone.

My dad would be at work. Even if he answered, he'd likely be unable to leave to rescue me.

Which left my mom. The woman I'd avoided for weeks. She wanted to know all about Luke and me. She didn't know we'd had a falling out—it would crush her. And after my failed wedding, I didn't want to do any more damage. Not so soon, anyway.

The tow truck finally came to a stop. As the driver got out to lower the car, I opened my door and jumped out. I didn't realize how far I was from the ground. My knees buckled when my feet hit the ground, and my entire body flopped into the dirt.

The man with blue coveralls and a thick brown ponytail gaped at me. "You—I—where'd you come from?"

"I've been in the car the entire time," I said. "Maybe you should check before you just tow a car away."

He stared at me like I was a ghost.

I stood and brushed myself off. "Be careful with my car. It shouldn't have been towed in the first place. I would have moved it if I had my keys, but Percy didn't wait around to let me explain."

The guy still gaped at me as I marched off toward the shack by the entrance gate.

I knocked on the window, and a woman peeked out. "Can I help you?"

"Can I use your phone, please?"

"We don't just let anyone use our phones, ma'am," she said. She was older and seemed like she meant business. She'd probably seen some crazy stuff in this position.

"I totally understand," I said. "It's just that I was towed here with my car, and now I need to get a ride to get my keys so I can come back here and pay to get my car out of jail."

She smiled. "You were towed here with your car?"

"Yep," I said. "I was asleep in the driver's seat when he hooked me up. Guess he didn't look in the windows."

She shook her head. "Sounds like you've had a bad day." She handed me the corded phone. "What's the number?"

I gave her my Mom's number and waited for the phone to ring.

It rang seven times before going to my mom's voicemail.

I handed the woman in the booth the receiver.

"Is there anyone else you want to call?"

"Yes," I said. "But I don't know their numbers."

She shook her head. "In my day, we memorized all our friends' numbers. It was the only way to get in touch with them. We didn't have these fancy smartphones that did everything for you. We weren't lazy like—"

The phone rang inside the booth, and she stopped ranting to pick it up.

"City impound," she said.

I could only see her eyes over the window ledge, but the longer she listened, the more her eyes widened and her eyebrows lifted.

Finally, she said, "Hold on, hold on. Who is this?"

"Who is this?" A voice I knew very well screamed through the receiver the woman was now holding six inches from her ear. "You called me. Tell me who you are."

The woman held the phone out to me. "I'm guessing it's for you."

I took the receiver, my face hot with embarrassment. "Mom? Mom!"

My mother stopped yelling. "Rylie? Is that you? Are you in jail? Is that why the police department is calling me?"

Stupid Caller ID telling her where the call was coming from.

"I'm not in jail," I said. "My car was towed, and I don't have my phone. Can you pick me up?"

"Can't you just drive here?"

"I don't have my keys either," I said. "Please, just come get me."

I gave her the address that the woman in the booth happily whispered to me and hung up.

"Your mom is a sassy one," the woman said with a smile. "I like that in a woman."

19

As I stood awkwardly at the booth, the guy who'd towed my car sped out of the gates.

"Is that who picked you up?" the woman asked.

"That's the one," I said. "When I got out of my car, he looked at me like he'd seen a ghost."

"I bet he did," she said. "He was probably out late with the guys last night and completely hungover."

I sensed a bit of frustration in her voice when she said that.

"Do you know him?"

"We dated once," she said. "He doesn't remember and doesn't even recognize me here. Just drives through and hands me his paperwork like we didn't sleep together."

Their age difference was startling, but who was I to judge?

"That's what started me on women," she said. "Though they haven't been much better now that I think about it."

The sound that made me cringe had me reaching for my pocket. Except I didn't have my phone.

"Oh, sorry," the woman said. "That's me. It's this stupid dating app where you don't add any pictures. You're supposed to fall for the other person's personality."

"Sounds good in theory."

"Sure, until you realize the only people who get on the app are uglies. Especially the women."

I didn't point out that she was one of those women. Or that I was.

"Did you meet that tow truck guy on the app?" I asked.

She shook her head. "Met him at a bar. But I recognized him from work. I thought he recognized me too, but apparently not." She huffed. "Have you ever tried a dating app?"

"Several," I said. "It actually helped me find my fiancé."

"Aww, that's sweet."

"Who is now my ex-fiancé."

She wrinkled her nose. "Not so sweet."

I shrugged.

"It seems like the dating pool on these apps is pretty limited," she said. "Like everyone is dating everyone else. Three of my friends—two girls and a guy—slept with the same guy in the same week through this app."

The first thing I would do when I got my phone back was delete that app. I didn't need that kind of drama in my life.

"There's my mom," I said. "Thanks so much for your help. I'll be back later to pick up my car."

"If you get back before five, I won't charge you," she said.

I smiled. "Thanks so much."

I didn't even get a smile or a hello when I got into my mother's car. "Now tell me why you don't have your phone or keys. That's dangerous, you know?"

I sighed. "I know. I left them in Nikki's car at the strip club, and she drove away."

"The strip club?" If my mom had been a Catholic, she would have made a sign of the cross over her chest. Instead, she closed her eyes in a silent prayer. "Have I taught you nothing? Was your upbringing so bad that you feel the need to go to strip clubs?"

"I wasn't going to the strip club for fun," I said. "I was going for work."

She nearly swerved off the road. "You've become a stripper? I thought nothing was worse than a park ranger, but you had to prove me wrong, didn't you? How will I tell your father? Or your nephews? What if your brother-in-law comes in and sees you naked? We all know he tends to go to those types of places."

"Eww, Mom, stop." I couldn't let her keep spiraling. "I'm not a stripper. I went back to being a park ranger."

She said nothing for several long seconds.

"Are you okay?" I asked.

"I never thought I'd say I was thankful you went back to being a park ranger, but here I am, thankful you went back to being a park ranger instead of becoming a stripper. You know, you really don't have the body for it, anyway. Men like their strippers to be super skinny with gigantic boobs. You're not big by any stretch of the imagination, but you have so many muscles. And your breasts are just not big enough. I'm sorry, honey, it had to be said."

"Did it?" I asked. "Did it really?" I kept myself from telling her that Percy said I could be a high-class stripper.

She shrugged. "How are things at the park?"

"Not great," I said. "I'm investigating five murders right now. And I suppose I should just tell you now, but I'm not really going back as a park ranger. I'm going back more as a hybrid ranger slash police officer."

"But you never trained to be an officer. That's just so dangerous."

"Better than being a stripper, though, right?" I asked. "At least my breasts aren't keeping me from this job."

She did not seem to appreciate my glibness. "This is not a joking matter. You are investigating five murders? That's so many. What happened while you were gone? And why the strip club? I didn't know there were any strip clubs in Prairie City."

I shouldn't have said a word. Now, I'd have to explain everything to her and swear her to secrecy.

Thankfully, I had a long drive from the impound lot to Nikki's house to do just that. At least she wasn't asking about Luke.

If Nikki's car hadn't been in her driveway, I might have lied to my mother just so she'd let me out of the car and leave. Turns out, telling her about what was going on was not the best course of action. She practically demanded I move home to live with her again so I could quit my job and become a librarian or something safe like that.

"I'll see you later," I said, getting out of the car. "Thanks for the ride."

"Think about what I said."

"Will do," I said. "Thanks again."

I closed the door before she could say anything else. I made a mental note never to tell her about my job again, knowing I'd forget, and we'd go through this exact conversation the next time a murder came up. For some reason, I just couldn't keep things to myself when it came to my mom.

My emotions came out when my fist met Nikki's front door.

She answered by throwing the door open with a face that said she was looking for a fight. "Why are you pounding on my door?"

"Why did you leave me without my purse in the strip club parking lot?"

"I didn't leave you . . ." Her face dropped. "Oh shit. I'm sorry."

"I got towed," I said. "And had to call my mother. Why didn't you call or come looking for me?"

"I did call," she said. "It went straight to voicemail. I figured you were mad at me and turned off your phone."

"Well, now I need you to get me to the impound lot before five so I can get Cherry Anne without being charged."

Oliver—Naked Guy—walked up behind Nikki and put

his head on her shoulder and his arms around her waist. "Hey, Rylie. What's up?"

"Good to see you fully dressed," I said. "I'm just trying to get your girlfriend to give me back my purse."

"Why'd you take her purse?" Oliver asked.

Nikki smiled up at him. "I didn't." She gave him a quick peck, and he released her. "At least, I didn't mean to."

"See you later, Oliver." I started to walk back down to her steps, but she hesitated. "What?" I asked. "Get your shoes, and let's go."

"It's just that my car is at the detailer," she said. "After those girls got in the backseat with all their oil and glitter and stuff, I had to get it cleaned up."

"Nik said you went to a strip club," Oliver said. "That's rad."

"It was for work," Nikki said. "Not pleasure."

"Isn't that your car right there?" I asked, bringing them back to the subject at hand and pointing to the car that looked exactly like hers in her driveway.

"It's my mom's," she said. "We like to have matching cars. She's letting me borrow it while mine's being cleaned."

"Let me guess, you didn't think to take my purse out of the car because you didn't think it was in there, so now it's trapped at the detailer, probably being pilfered through by some teenager."

She shrugged. "I'm sure no one is pilfering through it."

"Fine, then we'll go to the detailer, get my keys, and then go to the impound lot." I narrowed my eyes. "Unless you have another objection?"

She quickly shook her head. "Nope. I'll see you later, babe." She slipped her shoes on and gave Oliver one last kiss before following me down the steps.

20

Nikki tried to make small talk on the way to the detailer, but my ability to converse was broken. Between my frustration with her not caring about my whereabouts and my mother's over-caring about my life, I was all out of words for the day.

"It's only about three more exits up," she said. "We should have plenty of time to get your purse and get down to the impound lot before five."

As if on cue, her phone rang. On the car's touch screen, the name Harry Bryant popped up, along with his phone number.

"You jinxed it," I said. "He's going to tell us we must get to the station immediately."

"Hello?" Nikki said.

"Nikki, do you know where Rylie is? I've been trying to get a hold of her all day."

"She's with me," Nikki said. "And it's my fault she's been out of touch. Long story."

"No time," he said. "I need both of you at the station right away. I think we made a break in the case."

"Is it the author?" Nikki asked.

"Or her ex-husband?" I added. "Or maybe her ex-assistant, who her husband fell in love with and cheated on her with."

Nikki glanced over at me and raised her eyebrows.

"No," Harry said. "It has nothing to do with any of them. Just get to the station, and I'll explain."

"We need to get Rylie's purse first," Nikki said.

"No time," Harry said. "This is critical. Get here now."

Nikki looked at me with apologetic eyes.

"It's fine," I said when Harry hung up. "Let's go to the station. But you're paying for my impound fee."

She nodded so hard it looked like her head might fly off. "Of course. I can do that."

When we turned into the station, Harry was waiting outside for us.

"It must be urgent," I said.

Nikki parked the car, and we both hurried to meet him.

"We found a link between all five men," he said. "Each has been on the Just Personalities dating app."

My mouth went dry.

"A lot of people are on that app," Nikki said. "Rylie is too."

Harry looked at me questioningly, then shook his head. "That's neither here nor there," he said. "There's more. All of the men dated the same woman. Wanna know who that was?"

We both stared at him in anticipation.

"Henrietta Rose," he said. "They all dated the author who wrote the books and did the research and who killed them. We're going to pick her up now."

"You think the woman who has absolutely zero technology in her house and practically refuses to go out has joined a dating app and gone on multiple dates in the last month before she brutally murders them? I find that extremely hard to believe," I said.

"We're going over to discuss this with her," Harry said. "And we have a warrant to search the house. If we find nothing, we won't have enough to arrest her. Maybe someone is using her name for a fake profile. However, we can't actually ask any of the men if she's the one they dated because they're dead. Now, are you coming with me or not?"

Nikki nodded and looked at me.

Ugh, I had no choice. She was my ride. Plus, my curiosity was piqued. "Yeah, I'll go too."

Harry nodded once and led us out to his patrol car.

Nikki sat in the front, and I sat in the back, where people had probably puked and bled and sweated all over the seats. I pushed those thoughts away. I'd been in worse positions.

"Have you pinged the cell phone that has the app?" Nikki asked.

"It's in her house," Harry replied.

"Meaning either she did it, or someone close to her did." I considered this. "Have you thought about asking the app maker if they can find a list of people who dated the person behind the profile? Maybe someone is still alive and can identify the murderer."

"I have someone on the task," Harry said. "The problem is, the app maker is all about privacy. They have refused most of our requests."

"Can we find out if the phone pinged anywhere near where you found the bodies around the time the men might have died?" I asked.

"I believe that request is already in, but it would be a good reminder," Harry said. "Nikki, do you mind sending an email?"

Nikki pulled out her phone and started typing.

The street that had been dead the day before was now filled with more cars than the road was built to accommodate.

"What's going on?" Nikki asked.

"They all seem to lead to one place," Harry said.

I couldn't see much from the back seat, but I felt I knew where they were leading. Especially when I started seeing the news vans.

"We can't go any farther," Harry said. "We'll have to walk the rest of the way."

He parked the car right in the middle of the street behind a Channel 14 News van and opened my door.

Cameras and people had made a semi-circle around Bernie's house. Just beyond her property boundaries.

Both curious and unhappy neighbors stood outside to see what was happening. The unhappy ones practically sprinted to Harry when they saw his uniform, airing their complaints in loud voices.

"I have to get back to work," one man in a suit and tie said. "I should have never come home for lunch, but the wife is always nagging me to spend more time with her. Is there any way we can move these cars?"

Harry glanced over at the man. "I'm working on it."

When we reached the semi-circle of cameras, Harry shouted to reporters, "If you're parked in the middle of the street or blocking someone's driveway, you need to move now, or you will be towed."

A few people hurried off while most of the reporters shifted toward him, asking questions.

He held his hands up. "You'll need to talk to our Public Information Officer for specific questions."

I stopped to ask a reporter who wasn't actively recording, "Why are you here?"

"We were informed about Henrietta's books leading to several murders in the area," the woman said. "Would you like to do an interview?"

I shook my head. "Who told you about the murders?"

She looked down at her notes and shook her head. "An anonymous source."

"Come on, Rylie," Harry shouted back at me.

"Gotta go," I said before she could start asking me questions.

I hurried through the line of reporters and cameras and up the driveway. Bernie stood in her doorway, flanked by three security guards shouting at us. "Get off my property."

"We have a warrant," Harry said, holding up a piece of official-looking paper.

Her face paled. Then she noticed Nikki and me. Her face crumpled, and tears started down her cheeks as we hurried into her house.

Once the door was closed with the four of us inside, Bernie threw her arms around my neck. "This has been the worst day of my entire life."

Her dogs barked at my ankles, and part of me worried they might bite me. I patted Bernie on the back as she held on for an awkwardly long amount of time.

When she finally let go, Nikki and Harry both stared at me as if I should know what that was all about. Which I didn't.

"Let's go into the sitting room so we can chat," Bernie said. "I assume you're here to search the house."

"We're also here to talk to you," Harry said. "And your security guard, Uma."

"Did these two women not do a good enough job for you?" Bernie's voice was full of feministic rage.

Is that why she only killed men?

I shook my head. Innocent until proven guilty. She deserved the benefit of the doubt, just like anyone else. And just because she was a feminist didn't make her a murderer.

"I have full trust in these two women," Harry said. "They're the best in the business. However, we've recently received some new information that led us to this second round of questions."

"Go right ahead, but you won't be able to speak to Uma. She's out of the country," Bernie said. Being such a feminist, she sure was nicer to Harry than she had been to Nikki and me. Though I suppose she had just given me an enormous hug, so there was that.

"Out of the country?" Nikki asked. "That seems suspicious."

"She's had a vacation to Italy planned for months," Bernie said. "Check her tickets. She ordered them last November."

"We'll check into that," Harry said, slightly deflated that Uma wouldn't be available for questioning. "Do you have a cell phone?"

Bernie sighed. "I already told these two young women —I don't like technology. I don't have phones or smart watches or even a computer. I type everything on my type-writer, read my books in paper, and use locks instead of cameras. The only type of technology I permit in my house is that of those who visit and the communication things that my security guards wear in their ears."

"Why the increased security?" I asked. "Yesterday, there was only one guard outside and one inside. Now, there are three outside, two inside, and one at every window."

Bernie glanced out a window with a frightened expres-sion. "With all the murders happening, I thought I should watch out for myself in case the murderer wants to come after me."

Nikki's phone pinged, and she opened the email. After reading it while we watched intently, she clicked off the screen and looked up at Bernie. "How long do their shifts last?"

"Eight hours," Bernie said. "With breaks and such."

"And then they go home?" Nikki asked.

"I don't know where they go. They're not my friends. They're my staff."

"I mean, they don't stay here in the house with you?"

Nikki's tone was patient, but I could see her jaw tighten slightly once she was finished asking her question.

"The only person who stays in this house twenty-four hours a day is me, other than when I walk my dogs," Bernie said.

"And there are no devices inside your home that would be here for a full twenty-four hours?"

Bernie seemed to think about this for a moment, then said, "I don't even have a television that would be connected to the internet. I don't have internet service hooked up at all."

"I see," Nikki said. "Then can you explain the smart-phone that pings at this address twenty-four hours a day? Besides being at the exact locations when the men were murdered?"

21

B ernie gaped at Nikki. "I'd say you were lying through your teeth. I know police officers can lie when they interview someone. I've been a police officer. I've done the research."

"I'm not lying to you," Nikki said. "My tech guys just emailed me and said a phone used to access the Just Personalities dating app has been functional in your home for the last twenty-four hours. It was also at all the crime scenes during the murders."

"That's preposterous," Bernie said. "Dating app? Who would want to date this?"

She motioned up and down her body.

"The dating app is used without photos," I said. "It's to help find who you connect with on a deeper level."

"The only connection I need is with my pups," Bernie said. "Men are history in my life."

"Is there any reason you might have a cell phone in your house?" Harry asked. "Maybe one of your staff left theirs?"

"The way those things are practically glued to their hands, no, I can't imagine anyone left their device at my house. Plus, wouldn't it die eventually? What kind of phone stays fully charged for an entire twenty-four hours? Other than an actual corded phone?"

When we didn't respond, she continued, "Go ahead. You have a search warrant. Search. If you find a phone, get it out of here. It's not welcome."

With that, she sat back on the couch and crossed her arms over her chest.

"Nikki, stay with her," Harry said. "Rylie, come with me."

Nikki nodded while Bernie practically rolled her eyes at Nikki's presence.

Once we were out of earshot, I whispered to Harry, "If the phone has been on for the past twenty-four hours, it would have had to be plugged in. Let's check all the electrical outlets first. Also, check drawers, especially in the kitchen, bedrooms, and bathroom. Sometimes people put electrical outlets inside, so they don't have to have cords cluttering their counters."

Harry smiled and shook his head. "You haven't missed a beat, have you?"

I shrugged, unable to keep the growing smile off my face.

"Don't get cocky on me," Harry said. "We still have a killer to catch. Keep your eye out for other evidence while searching for the phone."

I nodded, and we headed in our separate directions.

He took the back hall of bedrooms and bathrooms while I took the kitchen, office, and more public spaces.

"Don't touch anything in my office," Bernie yelled when I walked into the cluttered mess of a space. "Unless you need it for the investigation, of course. Notice that I'm cooperating fully with your investigation."

Now that we had a warrant, she was.

It was surreal to be in the office of a woman whose work I admired but could also be a murderer. The typewritten pieces of paper were scattered on every surface. I read a few—for investigation purposes.

They all seemed to be outlines and garbled pieces of the books I'd already read. Almost like a stream of consciousness. I'd never considered how an author might write a book. I guess I just assumed they sat down at their computer and started at the beginning, telling the story until they got to the end. But from the pieces of paper in front of me, that seemed like an oversimplified assumption.

I did my best not to disturb the pages more than necessary. There wasn't a single electronic device in the office—every outlet was empty.

When I walked out, Bernie smirked. "Didn't find anything, did you?"

"Did you ever find that calendar?" I asked.

"Never did," Bernie said.

I'd checked the kitchen, dining room, office, and living spaces. The only place left was the garage. Since Harry wasn't finished with the bedrooms, I figured I'd get a head start searching there.

"Be careful out there," Bernie said, her voice changing from condescending to fright. "It's not terribly safe."

"What makes it unsafe?" Nikki asked.

I waited for her answer before going out.

"Between the angry ghost, the wonky roof, and the wobbly box towers, it's practically a kill zone."

The words kill zone sent a chill up my spine. If I walked out there, was I going to find her next victim? Or be her next victim?

Maybe she killed the men here and then took them to where the police had found them. It would make sense how she got the man in the water at the reservoir—she would definitely be strong enough to lift the small man.

But the person who ran from Antonio couldn't have been Bernie. If she had done this, she must have been working with someone. Like Uma.

"Are you going out there?" Nikki asked. "Or do you want me to?"

I realized I'd been holding the door handle and dazing into space. "I'll go. I'm not scared of ghosts, and I'll be careful with the boxes."

"But the roof—it might collapse," Bernie said, fear still on the edges of her voice, making her sound guilty.

"If the boxes are stacked high, they'll protect me." I pushed open the door, and a terrible smell hit my nose. It wasn't the smell of decomposition—at least not what I remembered decomposition to smell like—but it was bad nonetheless.

I found the light switch, and the sight illuminated before me was worse than I could have imagined. Bernie wasn't lying. This place was a death trap.

Boxes were not just stacked precariously on top of each other. They were practically crushing each other, and it looked like they might all fall down if anything touched one.

In addition, every type of weapon you could imagine lay strewn all around. Swords peeked out of boxes, guns—big and small—laid on the ground, ropes of various sizes and lengths hung from the ceiling made into nooses, and bottles with skulls and crossbones on them sat stacked on a shelf.

As I carefully made my way through the labyrinth of crazy, it only got crazier. Cages of all sizes were stacked beyond the first row of boxes. Chains and whips and other things you'd think would be more for erotica books than mysteries had their own special section. And against the very far wall were four metal barrels, just like the one the guy had been put in with acid before being thrown into the lake. They were the same color and everything.

My hope for Bernie not to be the killer was crushed.

I rewound my way through the garage to the house.

Harry met me at the door with wide eyes as he saw the garage.

"We're going to need the crime scene processing team out here right away," I said. "There's no way we can process all of this alone."

22

"I know what it looks like," Bernie said as she was being led to Harry's car in handcuffs, the reporters filming her every move. "Those are just props. They help me visualize the crimes. None of them have been used on another human or animal. They're just props."

"Typically, props aren't actual weapons," Nikki whispered. "But those looked pretty real."

"From what I could tell, they're real," I agreed. "But they all looked clean. I didn't see any blood."

"What was the smell?" Nikki asked.

"Who knows," I said. "Could be something rotting between the boxes. Or maybe it's a body. We'll only know once the crime scene team gets here."

As if on cue, a white van drove up the street, swerving around Harry's car, which was still parked in the middle of the road. Five men and women hopped out and pulled on gloves. Within minutes, they had a white tent set up around the front of the garage door to keep everything private from the cameras.

"Nikki, can you hang out here and relay any information they come across?" Harry said. "Rylie and I will head down to the station and see what we can find out about Bernie."

Nikki nodded. "Did you find the phone?"

As if he'd forgotten, Harry's eyes widened. "Good catch." He jogged back inside the house and came out moments later, clutching a brown paper bag in his hands. "Found it in one of the spare bedrooms inside a night-stand with a hidden outlet."

Pride swept over me for giving him a critical piece of information in finding the phone. Though he likely would have checked in nightstand drawers, anyway.

I slipped into the passenger seat, and Harry made a four-point turn right in the middle of the street before heading back out of the neighborhood.

"I swear," Bernie said from the back seat. "I didn't hurt anyone with those weapons. They were part of my research. The guns were only fired in my basement, so I could see what it felt like to shoot a gun. The knives never met a single piece of skin. Well, other than mine when they nicked me because I didn't know what I was doing. And I wouldn't even be strong enough to hoist one of those barrels when it was empty, let alone filled with base and a body."

Just the thought made my stomach churn. "Wait, did you just say a base? I thought the body was in there with an acid."

"If it was an acid," Bernie said, "it wasn't from my

book. Maybe it's from another author's series. Or maybe it's just a big coincidence."

I thought back to what I'd read. I was almost certain her book had said acid, but I'd have to go back and check. "Is that something you could have forgotten since it was the first book in the series?"

"I don't forget anything I write," Bernie said. "Acids are what the reader would expect. I like to go with the unexpected."

"Did you test what an acid and a base would do to human flesh before you used them in your book?" I asked. "I mean, if you don't like the internet, you would have had to try it, right?"

Harry shot me a glance. I probably wasn't supposed to be asking her questions in the police car, but he was wearing a body camera, so it wasn't like the conversation wasn't being recorded.

"I don't like the internet, but there are other ways of researching than typing something into the Google. Like reading books. And though I like to put my hands on weapons before I write about them, I'd never hurt another person for research's sake."

I stopped the questioning so I didn't make Harry mad. It was shocking that Bernie was talking to me at all since she had been notified of her rights—one of them being the right to an attorney.

When we walked into the station, Harry started doing all his paperwork and fingerprints while I stood to the side and watched.

"Are you Rylie Cooper?" a female officer I'd never seen before asked.

"I am," I said.

"I think this is yours," she said, handing me my purse. "Nikki asked me to pick it up and get it to you ASAP."

I almost asked why this officer was okay doing Nikki's bidding but left it alone.

"Thank you so much," I said as my phone vibrated in my purse.

She nodded and walked away with a smile.

I had three messages—one from Mom, one from Nikki, and one from Antonio.

I opened Antonio's first.

I am very sorry about the date. If you give me a chance, next time will be better. I promise.

Something stirred inside me. This time, it didn't feel like dread. It felt like hope. I sent a quick text back.

Let's try again soon.

Mom's message was just asking if I'd gotten my car back. I told her no but that I would soon.

Nikki's message was a picture of the garage from the perspective of the open garage door.

What had looked like a mess from the door to the house now looked like a carefully constructed laboratory of sorts from the big door.

Everything was labeled on the side facing the street. Some boxes were marked with a weapons list, and others were labeled with book titles. They'd been strategically organized based on the book they correlated with.

My mind went back to Bernie's office and how messy it was. How did she have such an organized—if rather dangerous—garage laboratory?

Have you found a computer? I'm having a hard time believing she never uses one. And thanks for getting my purse back.

I sent my text, then headed to the interrogation room.

The same female officer who brought me my purse stood beside a male officer outside the door. The man opened the door to the room with a two-way mirror to watch and listen to interrogations without being inside.

Bernie sat in a metal chair, her hands cuffed and chained to a bar that spanned the length of the metal table and bolted to the concrete floor.

Nothing about the room was welcoming. It meant business.

The two officers stood next to me but said nothing. We watched as Harry entered the room, and Bernie glanced up at him with tears in her eyes.

"Can you explain what this is?" He slid what looked like a printed picture of the one Nikki had just sent via text.

"It's my garage," she said.

"It's very organized."

"Courtesy of my many assistants. They hated cleaning it, but it was necessary if I was to find anything."

That made sense. She wasn't the one cleaning it. But it also meant too many fingerprints to process anything worthwhile.

"How did you know where things were?" Harry asked.

"I have an inventory in my office," she said. "Everything is accounted for, and if I need a prop for a book signing—not that I do those anymore—but if I did, I'd have the proper items to bring along."

"Such as guns and knives?"

"I didn't take the weapons with me to the signings," she said. "That would have been incredibly irresponsible."

"How long have you been writing, Ms. Herrigarta?"

"I've been creating stories since I could talk," she said. "My mother would write them down. She kept dozens of journals with my stories. When I finally learned how to write for myself, I took over.

"I started publishing as a child. My father thought it would make them rich—he was a bit of a prick and wasn't thrilled when no one wanted to read my books. It probably had something to do with the fact that a little girl wrote books about murder and blood and gore. He tried to get me to write about unicorns, fairies, and all the things girls were supposed to enjoy. But I was always intrigued with mysteries."

"How many books do you have published?"

"Hundreds," Bernie said. "Though most are under my legal name. As far as Henrietta Rose's books, there have been about thirty."

"When did your books become your primary source of income?"

"What does this have to do with the murders?" Bernie asked. "Not that I mind talking about my career, but how is this getting you any closer to solving the case?"

"I know you have some experience in interrogation,"

Harry said, "but I need to do this my way. Can you please answer the question?"

Bernie let out a large sigh. "My books have supported me since I was fifteen—the day my father kicked me out of the house." Tears welled in her eyes again, and Harry handed her a tissue. "I wrote them by hand and had them photocopied in print shops. Every time I sold a book, I'd buy just enough food and water to keep me alive and put the rest into making more copies."

"What did your mother think about your father kicking you out of the house?"

"My mother would have murdered him if she had known. But she was dead—he killed her."

23

I glanced at the officer next to me, whose face looked about as shocked as mine. Bernie had just accused her father of murdering her mother.

That kind of childhood trauma could be a massive indicator pointing to Bernie being a serial killer.

"Why do you believe your father may have killed your mother?" Harry said, flipping through his notes. This had obviously taken him aback.

"You won't find anything about it in your records," Bernie said. "I grew up in rural England. My father was in law enforcement. There was no investigation."

Harry stopped shuffling his paperwork and looked up at Bernie. "If you can, will you tell me what happened?"

Bernie sucked in a deep breath. "I don't know why it's so hard. I've been waiting decades for a police officer to care about what happened to my mother—to ask me what I saw that day. I've practically memorized it." She closed her eyes and cleared her throat. "It was my fault they started arguing. Not every time, but I was to blame on this sweltering summer day.

"I was fourteen—on the eve of my fifteenth birthday—and my mother asked what I wanted as a gift. I told her I simply wanted a share of the royalties from my books so I could start saving for college.

"It was something we'd discussed in whispers before. She knew my father would never stand for it. He was old-fashioned, thinking any money made in his household belonged to him. But on this day, I worked up the courage to speak my mind.

"When my mother smiled and nodded in agreement, he hit her so hard across the jaw that she went uncon-scious." She stopped and looked down at her hands. "If only he would have left her there, she might have come back to us—to me."

Harry waited in silence while Bernie gathered her thoughts.

"He'd had a lot to drink, like most days, which made him angrier. I should have known better than to stir up trouble, but I thought I'd take a gamble since my birthday was approaching. My gamble cost my mom her life. He went inside, got a pillow, and held it over her face until her chest stopped moving."

Tears flowed in rivers down Bernie's face, matching my own.

"He waited to call it in until the next day. He acted like he'd woken up to find her like that—claimed she'd fallen and hit her jaw on the stove while baking my cake. If the bobbies had simply looked around and realized there was no cake, they would have caught him in the lie, but they took his word for gold. He was one of them, after all."

Harry winced.

"It was my birthday, but the only person who cared was gone," Bernie said, wiping the tears from her face. "Once the bobbies had taken my mother's body and left the scene, my father told me if I ever asked for another penny of the money my books had earned, he'd do the same to me as he'd done to her.

"I stayed in a state of shock for a week or two. This part's a blur now. One day, when he came home, and there was nothing left to eat in the refrigerator—my mother did all the shopping and cooking—he told me to get out of his house. I was just a mooch and would bankrupt the both of us.

"As far as I know, he still makes measly royalties from my early books."

The room was silent. I was certain Harry hadn't expected all this to come out in an interrogation about current murders. And as far as I knew, there wasn't anything he could do about a murder in England decades ago.

He sucked in a breath and said, "I'm very sorry you had to go through all that."

Bernie wiped her eyes and squished her nose back and forth without actually blowing it. "It made me who I am today."

The officer next to me turned and looked at me wide-eyed. He was probably thinking the same thing as I was— it could have made her into a murderer herself. A serial killer.

"Would you mind continuing? How did you get to the United States? And when did you become a household name?"

"As I said, I sold books like my life depended on it—which it did. I had every woman in my village skipping their womanly duties to read the next book in my handwritten series. They were on the edge of their seats while their husbands complained of their laziness. It wasn't great for them, but I made enough money by the time I was eighteen to go to college in the States.

"I paid my tuition in full with cash on the first day of orientation. I knew it was the only way I'd stay true to my goal of finishing. Especially with all the things you can buy in America. But I learned to manage without them just like I do today.

"Eventually, I became a creative writing teacher at that same college. Many of my students have had very prolific careers themselves."

She had made quite the legacy for herself. I couldn't help but smile at her story.

"In between classes, I'd write," she continued. "I never spent more than I made, and I made sure the extra went back into my business. That is until I met Percy."

Her demeanor shifted from triumphant to angry.

"He acted like a feminist at heart with his club and all. I thought he was all about empowering women. I guess that didn't include his own wife. He spent a good chunk of the money I'd saved, setting my career back years.

"When I refused to use credit to continue publishing books, he started fooling around with my assistant and ended up leaving me for her. As far as I know, they're still together."

"How about we discuss your ex-husband?" Harry said. "When my other officers spoke with you yesterday, you told them that Percy had been trying to get more money from you. That he'd been at your house recently. But he told them he hadn't been to your house since the two of you divorced. Can you perhaps clear up the confusion?"

She shook her head. "I'm sorry, you seem nice enough, but I'd like to speak with Rylie, please." She looked directly at the mirror, seemingly meeting my gaze. "The rest of this story needs to go to her."

24

I'd never formally interrogated anyone. I didn't have the training for it. But apparently, that didn't matter. Harry led me into the room. When Bernie made a big enough fuss, he left the two of us alone together.

"Here are the keys to get out of the room." He handed me a key ring. "There will be someone outside the door if you knock, but just in case."

"In case what?" I whispered with my back turned to Bernie, hoping she couldn't hear me. "She's handcuffed to the table. Her legs are shackled together. I don't think she's going to hurt me."

"Don't underestimate people," Harry said. "And you can't always think the best of them."

I wasn't about to think the worst about people, either.

He left the room, and I sat facing Bernie.

"Did you hear all that?" she asked.

I nodded. "I'm so sorry you had such a horrible childhood. It's impressive how you beat all the odds."

She gave me a small smile. "Thank you. I think I would have liked to have you as a student."

"Nah," I said. "I'm a horrible writer. Not much creativity in this head."

She laughed. "I can pull the creativity out of a turnip. Trust me. I would have had fun with you."

I could almost feel Harry's eyes on my back. I needed to get on with the questioning. "Can you tell me about the inconsistencies in your statement versus Percy's?"

"What did he tell you?"

"We went to the club last night," I said. "He didn't want to speak with us, but when he did, he said you have a restraining order against him and that he went to your house to discuss something, but not money. He said he makes plenty of money with the club and doesn't need any of yours."

She shook her head. "He would say that."

"But you told me the exact opposite, so which is the truth?"

"Isn't the truth subjective?" Bernie asked.

"Not really," I said. "Sure, different people have different points of view, but what happened happened. Either he wants your money, or he doesn't."

"He was at my house. He broke the restraining order."

"What did he go there to talk about?"

"I don't wish to speak of that."

"Why didn't your security stop him at the door?"

"He can be very persuasive."

"So, you let him in because he had something to tell you, but you won't tell me what he said."

"It's not important." She looked down at the cuffs around her wrists. She was lying.

"You know what I think?" I asked. "I think it is important. I think he came over to talk to you about the murders. Maybe the two of you are working together, killing these guys."

"Percy and I can barely be in a room alone without murdering one another, and you think we're on some murderous team?" This time, she looked me straight in the eyes. "We aren't killing people together. What he came over to discuss has nothing to do with this case."

This line of questioning was getting me nowhere. I turned around and looked at the mirror.

"Ask me who I think did it," Bernie whispered.

I turned around and shook my head, trying to keep the smile off my lips. She was helping me—teaching me—how to do my job. "Who do you think did it? Other than Percy, because I know that will be your first answer."

"If I can't say Percy, then I'd have to say it's a crazy fan," she said.

Going after all her crazy fans would be a wild goose chase.

When the door opened, I had never felt so relieved in my life.

Harry walked in with a folder of what looked like photographs. He sat in the chair next to me. "I'd like to talk to you about the events of the murders."

"I already told you I'll only talk to her," Bernie said.

"I'm not leaving," I assured her. "But you can trust Harry to do his job to the best of his ability."

"He can lie to me," she said.

"So can I," I said. "But I won't."

"I know you won't. That's why I want to talk to you."

"Okay, talk to me. He'll ask the questions, and you can relay your answers to me. Does that work?"

She shrugged. "We'll play it by ear."

Harry pulled out five photos of the people murdered—photos of them alive.

"Do you recognize any of these men?" I asked before Harry had to. I figured if I could ask the questions, it might make things go smoother.

She flipped through them one by one, studying the faces. When she reached the last one, she shuffled them up and looked through a second time.

"I'm pretty certain I've seen this man," she handed us the photo of the one who—if I recalled correctly—had been the gunshot victim that looked like a suicide but wasn't.

"Where do you think you've seen him?" I played along with her. If she were lying and had killed them, it would only make sense that she'd just pick one.

"I think he was at my house—maybe a gardener or something. I can't keep track of all the people I hire to keep things in working order. That's usually a task for my assistant."

"Your assistants seem to do a lot of work for you," I said. "Do you think one of them could be responsible for the murders?"

She considered this for a moment again and then shook her head. "They were all too stupid. They probably haven't even read my books—in fact—I know most of them haven't."

"The next pictures I'm about to show you are more gruesome," Harry warned.

"I think I can handle it," Bernie said. "It's not like I haven't seen all this stuff during my research."

Harry laid the pictures of the victims below their alive portraits so that Bernie could look.

She held it together for the first couple, but when he laid down the one of the false suicide gunshot—the man Bernie thought she might have seen—she started crying again.

"I'm sorry," she said. "I don't know why I'm so emotional today. I never cry like this. Murder is part of my job. I've hardened myself to it. Or at least I thought I had."

I handed her a tissue, and she dabbed at her eyes before wadding it up into a ball in her hands.

She closed her eyes and cleared her throat before opening them and taking a fresh look at the photos. "Let's go through them one by one. Tell me about the murders."

"I don't have all the details," I said. "But we can trust Harry to give it to us straight."

He didn't indicate in any way that he would give it to us straight. Instead, he started in with the descriptions.

"The first murder was the man in the barrel of acid," he said. "This young man messaged you via the Just Personalities app—"

"I don't have a smartphone," Bernie interrupted. "And I wasn't on any dating app. If you couldn't tell, I don't much like men."

"I thought this might come up," Harry said, pulling several other photos from the folder. "These are pictures of the phone we found in one of your guest bedrooms. If we could figure out the password, I'd guess it has the Just Personalities app on it."

He put photos on the table showing the phone in the nightstand drawer.

Bernie swallowed hard, causing an actual gulping sound. "I think I need to call my lawyer."

We should have known she'd lawyer up the minute we put her in a corner. And the phone evidence was a definite corner.

"We need to take prints off the phone to see if she touched it," I said. "And the dresser drawer handle and the charging cube."

"We're on it," Harry said. "But preliminary findings are pretty minimal. It seems whoever did this was meticulous about fingerprints."

"Did you see that woman's office?" I asked. "Nothing about her is meticulous."

"Except she would be the first person to know not to leave fingerprint evidence."

"And she'd be the first to know that a cell phone is trackable," I said. "Do you think she's stupid enough to have carried that phone with her only to the places where those men were killed and then left it practically in the open at her house for the police just to stumble in and find?"

He hesitated a moment at this thought.

"We need to check on the father," I said as we walked out of the hallway and into the lobby. "If he's in the States, he might have come to intimidate Bernie. And try to get Uma on the phone, at least."

"Oh, thank God." June practically tackled me in a hug. "Have you seen Bernie?"

"Bernie is in a cell awaiting her time with the judge," Harry said.

June let me go. "The judge?"

"Bernie has been arrested for murder," Harry said. "She's being held without bond and cannot have visitors."

"Murder?" June asked. "You think she killed those people?"

"You thought so yesterday," I said.

"I was just frustrated with her," June said. "She sends me all these stupid typewritten or worse—handwritten— notes that I can barely decipher and she wants me to complete everything on the list while she forgets what she put on the list and doesn't care whether I did it or not until she does care that I forgot something and demands to see the list and then realizes all the things I forgot, then she has a fresh list of things to do too."

"That sounds challenging," I said, using the same tone my sister used when she talked my little nephews off the edge. "Maybe you should take this time while she's incarcerated to take a break. Maybe go to the spa or take a nap?"

"I can't go to the spa or take a nap," June's voice intensified, and a few of the people in the lobby turned to see what the commotion was about. "We have a book that needs to be uploaded, and I don't have the passwords. If I don't get it uploaded by midnight, the next book will not go out, and we'll lose all our preorders—so many preorders since the case was featured on the news—besides a host of other problems."

"And Bernie has the passwords?"

"She's the only one who accesses the account. It's something she doesn't trust anyone else to do."

"I thought she didn't use computers?"

"This is the only time she does," June said. "With a great deal of help from me."

"Bernie said she was working on the outline for the next book. Maybe she already uploaded it," I said. "Maybe she figured out how to do it herself."

"She didn't," June shouted. "She couldn't have. She didn't have it to upload yet."

Harry looked at her. "Who had it?"

"The editor," she said. "Her editor was putting the finishing touches on it like she always does right before Bernie uploads it. I've tried to get her to do this ahead of time, but she won't. Please, I need the passwords, or all our work—all her work—will be for nothing."

Part of me wanted to help, but the more logical part said, "I can't get you that password. If that book goes public before we catch the killer, we might have another murder on our hands."

"If you think Bernie did it, and she's in jail, how would she murder someone else?" June looked like she was about to get down on her hands and knees and beg. "Please get me that password."

"Are you certain Bernie couldn't have uploaded this

herself without you knowing?" Harry asked.

June sighed. "She uses my computer. She doesn't have a computer of her own. It's the only thing she does on the computer, and it's only because she's such a control freak. She doesn't trust anyone with her money, her business, or her dogs."

"Why don't you wait out here, and we'll try to get an answer for you by midnight," Harry said.

June sat in one of the plastic chairs next to a guy with tattoos over every bit of exposed skin, including his face. She looked so tiny and frail next to him. I felt horrible for her. She was just trying to do her job. If she didn't get that book out on time, and it cost Bernie all those preorders, she'd likely be fired.

I'd have to tell Bernie it wasn't June's fault. Make her see that it would have worked out better if she had trusted someone else with her passwords.

Plus, I had a feeling people wouldn't care if it didn't release on its preorder date—they'd be clamoring to get their copies regardless of when it came out. I knew I would.

An idea popped into my head. "What if I read it?"

"What if you read what?" Harry said, his face practically buried in the file with the case information.

"The book that's supposed to release," I said. "What if I read it and we can get to where the next person might be murdered? Then we release the book and see what happens. It might be a good way to catch the person responsible."

Harry thought about this for a moment. "Is this just your way of getting your hands on the book early?"

"Doesn't hurt." I smiled, then sighed. "No, it's not my way to get my hands on the book early. I think this might be the best idea we could come up with."

After a minute, Harry nodded. "See if you can get a copy from the assistant. If not, we'll try to get a warrant." He looked at his watch. "Do you think you can read it before midnight?"

"Give me a couch and some snacks, and I'll be good to go," I said. "Plus, we only need to know who is murdered, how they're murdered, and where they're murdered. Usually, that stuff comes pretty close to the beginning of the book."

"While you're working on that, I'll see if Nikki can get the passwords out of Bernie's grasp."

I considered this for a minute. "What if she doesn't want to give them up? What if she doesn't care whether the book is published or not?"

"Were you not just in there?" Harry said. "It seems to me like she cares more about her success than just about anything."

He had a point.

"Keep looking for the dad while I read."

"Do you think the dad has come to the States after all these years just to intimidate his daughter?" Harry asked. "Why now?"

"Her career only took off with this series," I said. "Maybe he somehow figured out she was writing under a pen name and decided to exact his revenge."

"I'll look into it, but it's pretty far-fetched." He walked into his office while I turned back down the hallway to talk to June.

26

"You want me to let you read the book before it's released to the public without Bernie's consent?" June shook her head. "I can't do that. Bernie doesn't let anyone read her books. Not even her assistants."

She seemed slightly bitter about this.

"Not that I'd care. I don't like mystery novels, anyway."

She did strike me as more of a romance type.

"Look, Nikki is going to get the password from Bernie, but this is the only way we'll let you use that password to publish the book. I need to read it first so we can be prepared to catch the killer," I said. "And if you don't give it to me, I'll have to get a warrant, which will take days, and you won't get the passwords in time to upload the book tonight."

She glanced at the clock on the wall. "You'll read the entire thing in less than six hours?"

"I'm going to read the parts I need in less than two," I

said. "You'll have plenty of time and bandwidth to upload that book before midnight."

She stood there with a look of indecision on her face. "Fine," she said, sitting and pulling her laptop from her bag. "But you better tell Bernie this was your idea. If she finds out I willingly handed over her manuscript, she'll kill me." She looked up with wide eyes. "Not literally. She wouldn't literally kill me."

"It's okay," I said. "Can you somehow send it so it will come to my reader app on my phone?"

She typed and clicked for a few minutes. "What's your email address?"

I told her.

"There it should be in your inbox. Just click on the link, and it'll automatically go to the app." She glanced at the clock again. "Time is ticking. Go read."

I walked back down to Harry's office. "Got the book. Where can I read it?"

"I'll set you up in the lounge and make sure no one bothers you."

I'd asked for a couch and snacks. The couch was a seventies-style yellow flowered couch with springs that poked through the fabric. "Where are the snacks?"

"They're forthcoming," he said. "You can start reading without them, right?"

"I suppose," I said, sitting on the least spring-filled part of the couch and realizing it wasn't uncomfortable. "I'll find you when I'm finished."

"Just text me. I might not be in my office."

"Perfect," I said. "Don't forget about the snacks."

He waved a hand in the air before walking out and

closing the door behind him. A few minutes later, I thought I heard someone writing on the door, which was probably Harry making a handmade keep-out sign.

The book started slow—much slower than her books usually did. In fact, it was almost hard to keep my focus as my eyes started to close.

I stood from the couch and started pacing to keep myself awake. I wasn't a writer, but that didn't mean I couldn't tell when something had or hadn't been edited. And if this was edited, Bernie needed to fire her editor.

I pushed past the obvious misuses of there, their, and they're and finally came to the murder.

I gasped when I realized who was dead.

It was the cop the main character had been so close to dating in the last book. They'd kissed a couple of times throughout the series, but she'd finally figured out how to be in a relationship, and now he was dead.

My eyes welled up with tears as I tried not to speed through without noticing the details of the murder. That's why I was reading this, not because I was a super fan who loved all of Henrietta's books. At least the books in this series.

He'd been shot. Right between the eyes.

The main character was sobbing. The other police officer characters were sobbing. I was sobbing.

"Are you okay?" A quiet voice said from the door.

I turned to find Antonio standing with a massive bag of snacks in his hands.

I rushed to him and threw my arms around his neck. "He died. The guy in the book died. Her love interest."

Antonio held me tight with both of his arms. "It is okay. It is just a book."

"But she's so sad," I said, my voice muffled in his shirt. "And it means the next murder will be a police officer."

"I brought you snacks," Antonio said. "And your car."

I pulled away and looked up at him. "How? You did?"

"I know some people over at the impound lot, and your mom found a spare set of keys at your house when she went to feed Fizzy." He put the spare set of keys in my hand.

"Thank you," I said. "You didn't have to do that."

"I wanted to," he said. "You have had a rough few weeks. After that awful date, I had to make it up to you."

"The date wasn't awful," I said.

"Okay, that awful kiss," he said with a small smile as he rubbed the back of his neck in embarrassment.

"Yeah, what happened there?" I asked. "Our first kiss was so . . ."

"Magical."

I smiled. "Magical is the right word for it."

"Maybe we can only have magical kisses when they are forbidden."

"Well, I don't exactly want one of us to have to cheat to be able to kiss each other. That seems a bit back-asswards."

He laughed. "I'm willing to give it another shot if you are."

"Cheating?" I asked.

"Not cheating," he said. "Kissing."

I nodded, and before my brain could make any sense of his movement, I let myself fall into his arms. His kiss was magical once again. All the sadness from the book washed away. The main character would get her happy ending, eventually. But I was getting my happy ending now. Or my happy beginning.

When he pulled away, I resisted the urge to grab him tight and force him to keep kissing me.

I opened my eyes to find him smiling.

"The magic is back."

27

Antonio sat on the pokey spring side of the couch while I quickly finished the book and snarfed down a good portion of the snacks. He rubbed my feet and smiled every time we made eye contact.

Once I finished the book, I stood and stretched. I might not have gotten the full effect of Henrietta's words, but I knew enough about the plan to work.

"Why don't you take my car home," I said to Antonio. "I'm probably going to be a few more hours. And either Nikki can bring me to pick up my car, or I'll call you to pick me up."

Antonio smiled and leaned in for another kiss. His lips were soft and gentle. "Call me, and I will come get you."

I handed him the keys with a smile and watched him walk away.

When he was out of sight, I texted Harry.

I finished the book.

His response came back almost immediately.

We're in the interrogation room.

I wandered down the winding hallways until I finally found the room. When I knocked, the door opened immediately.

Inside were Harry, Nikki, Bernie, and June.

"Can we upload it?" June asked.

Bernie didn't seem to care one way or another, but I assumed since they were sitting with a laptop open, she'd agreed to give them the passwords when things were ready to go.

"I need to speak with Rylie for one moment before we move forward," Harry said. "Let's go in the hall."

He knocked, and the door opened.

"What'd you find out?" he asked.

"It's an officer," I said. "A police officer gets shot between the eyes at the top of a tower overlooking a lake."

"Close range or from a sniper?"

"Close," I said. "Burn marks on the forehead skin close."

"And it wasn't a suicide?"

"No, it was his jilted lover," I said. "But he was about to start dating the main character in the previous book, so it was really sad."

"Anything else of note?" he asked. "A second murder?"

"Her books only have one," I said. "Do most have more than one?"

"We can talk reading later," he said. "We have a case to solve. Go in and tell them they can upload the file. I'll start assembling a team. Where is there a tower that over-looks a lake in Prairie City?"

"At Alder Ridge," I said. "Right in the plaza. It's the only one I can think of, but you might call Dusty and ask if there are any in the rural."

He nodded once and walked away while the officer at the door opened it for me to go back inside.

"Now?" June asked, checking her phone for the time. "Can we send it?"

"Can I talk to you for one minute before you do?" I asked her. "In private?"

I needed to tell her about the grammar mistakes the editor had missed before she hit send, but I didn't want her or the editor to get into trouble with Bernie. June likely couldn't fix the slow start—only Bernie could do that—but she could fix the their, there, they're problem.

"What?" June asked.

"I found some mistakes you might want to fix before you upload it," I whispered. "Just little ones."

Her eyes widened. "If you tell Bernie, I'll be out of a job. I recommended this editor. It's her first job. Please don't tell Bernie."

"I'll email them to you," I said. "Then I'll distract her while you fix them, and then she can type in the pass-word, and you can upload the fixed file."

She nodded so hard that her hair fell over her face. "It's just grammar, though, right? I wouldn't know the first thing about fixing one of Bernie's books."

"Just grammar," I assured her.

"Great," she said. "Thank you so much."

She hurried back to the table while I sent the mistakes

I found through email. As I approached the table, I heard the ping of the email arriving on her computer. She smiled at me quickly before starting the fixes.

"What are you doing?" Bernie asked. "You're not changing anything, are you? I want it uploaded exactly how it is."

She couldn't possibly want it uploaded with grammar mistakes, and June wasn't fixing anything about the actual book. "You know I'm not a writer," June said, glancing up at Bernie, then at me to work on the distraction.

"Bernie," I said, "do you think there's any way your father might be in the States?"

Bernie's eyes widened, and even June momentarily stopped what she was doing.

"No, why?" Bernie asked.

"After you told us about what he did, we wondered if perhaps he got wind of your fame and is now doing this to taunt you."

"You don't think I killed them?" Bernie asked. "Then why am I still in handcuffs?"

"Evidence," I said. "All the evidence points to you right now. But if you think he might be in the country, he'd definitely be someone we'd want to look into."

She paused, glancing down at her hands in contemplation. Finally, she looked back up at me. "I didn't want to tell you before, but that puzzle note you gave me—I think it's from him."

"You do?" I asked.

Bernie nodded. "*What's in a name?* That's what it said. He was a big Shakespeare fan, and it would make sense that he sent me that note since I'm using a pseudonym."

"Why didn't you tell us that at that point?" I asked.

"He's not someone you mess with," Bernie said. "And if he's in the country, he's not just here to kill people like in my books—he's here to kill me."

"Maybe he's just trying to intimidate you," I said.

"Well, it worked," Bernie said. "That's why I upped my security after your first visit. I practically begged Uma to stay home, but she refused. As I said, my staff members aren't exactly my friends and don't pretend to be."

I glanced at June to see if she reacted to Bernie's admission, but she just continued working on the manuscript.

"Once you hit send, how long will it take for the book to get into people's hands?" I asked.

Nikki's gaze went back and forth between us, her eyes half-closed with exhaustion.

"It releases in two days—forty-eight hours from the stroke of midnight," Bernie answered. "And after that, you'll know I'm not the killer."

"You're not going to bond out?" Nikki asked.

Bernie shook her head. "I've slept in worse places than a jail cell. I want to prove it's not me killing anyone."

"But what if no one is caught? What if the killer knows you're in jail and decides not to go through with it until you're out?" I asked. "Especially since if you didn't do it, they're really trying to frame you."

Bernie shrugged. "Then maybe I'll just stay here until they kick me out. I could use a break from writing, anyway. My fingers hurt from that typewriter."

"All ready for your password," June said, shooting Bernie a frustrated look. I couldn't imagine how hard it must be for her to deal with a boss who acted like a greedy two-year-old.

Bernie turned the computer away so June couldn't see it, typed her password in super-fast, and then clicked on the button that declined to save the password on the computer.

June took back over, with Bernie watching like a hawk as she clicked and typed and clicked and typed until a look of relief washed over June's face. "Fifteen minutes to spare."

Bernie reached over and took quick control of the computer, logging June out of the account and closing the window before leaning back in her chair. "I'd like to go to my cell now. I'm rather tired."

Harry sent both Nikki and me home for the night. I didn't have the heart to bug Antonio so quickly after he'd left. He'd probably just settled into his bed.

Fizzy was quick to greet me with his wagging tail and floppy tongue. "How you doing, buddy?" I scratched behind his ears as he wiggled in excitement. "Sorry I've been out for so long. Mom let you outside and fed you, though, right?"

I glanced up to find my apartment tidied and a note propped up on the counter against a vase of beautiful daisies.

"Looks like that's a yes."

I smelled the flowers and read the note.

I'm so proud of you for going back to work. Even if it's dangerous. Food's in the fridge. Love, Mom

That might have been one of my mom's nicest letters. I

slipped it inside my purse for safekeeping. She had the most beautiful handwriting that someday I'd miss.

My eyes went misty, and I had to clear my throat to brush away the emotion.

Fizzy nuzzled the side of my leg.

"I'm okay, buddy," I said. "Just tired and emotional." I thought about the food in the fridge. "And hungry."

A whole pan of my mother's famous lasagna sat proudly amidst the fully stocked shelves. I cut myself a piece and heated it in the microwave before settling on the sofa with the first book in Bernie's series.

I flipped open the cover and started reading while shoving bite after bite in my mouth. The writing was so different. I couldn't shake the thought that maybe June was releasing Bernie's book too soon. Bernie probably usually did a final check of the books after the editor and before sending them to be published.

Either that or Bernie was losing her touch.

I grabbed the second book and read the beginning. Another strong beginning.

Same with the third, fourth, and fifth books.

Hopefully, I was the only one who noticed the difference. Mainly because this could be Bernie's most popular book to date. And if it wasn't as good—which, in my opinion, it wasn't—then people might stop reading her books altogether.

I finished the lasagna and let Fizzy lick the plate before heading to bed. I needed sleep.

The first thing I did when I woke up the next morning was text Ursula.

I'm coming back.

She texted back almost immediately.

When?

I smiled and replied.

Now. Today. Yesterday. I'm sorry it took me so long.

I would have waited longer, but I'm glad you're back. Come see me as soon as possible. Nikki may have given you a heads up about the new division, but I'd like to tell you about the specifics.

Does today work? We're in a holding pattern until the next book releases.

Today's perfect. Text me before you come so I can clear my schedule.

I sent back a thumbs-up emoji and then moved on to my next contact—Antonio.

Wanna pick out a new pet with me today?

His response didn't come back right away, so I shut the phone off and jumped in the shower.

By the time I was finished, his response was waiting for me.

I'm off at two. Should we go then?

Perfect.

Also, I dropped your car off in the parking lot in case you needed it today. Dusty gave me a ride back. I took the keys since you have one set. I will give you the spare set when I see you.

I sent him a smile emoji.

Thanks so much. You're the best.

No, you are. See you at the reservoir at 2?

Can't wait!

I clutched the phone to my chest as butterflies seemed to flutter around inside. I hadn't felt this enamored since I'd first started dating Garrett.

* * *

Cherry Anne sat in the parking lot in the exact spot where I always parked. Antonio had only been to my apartment a handful of times, meaning he'd either taken notice or had an excellent memory.

I wore a pair of my nicest jeans and a long-sleeved dark

blue blouse. I wanted to look nice enough to talk to Ursula but also pretty enough to be on a day date with Antonio since I likely wouldn't have much time to go home and change before heading to Alder Ridge.

Ursula gave me the biggest smile I think I'd ever seen on her face when I walked into her office. "It's so good to have you back."

"It's good to be back," I said, sitting in the chair across the desk from her. "Thanks for being so patient with me."

"I didn't want to believe it at first, but you are a real asset to this department. Which is why we're giving you your own division." She pulled out a three-ring binder and handed it to me.

On the front, it said Hybrid Ranger-PD Division Policies and Procedures. Below that, it said Division Leader Rylie Cooper.

"I'm sorry. What does Division Leader mean?"

"It means you're the boss," Ursula said. "I'm guessing Nikki kept that part to herself."

Nikki had always been one step ahead of me. We'd competed for the same position once, and she'd gotten it. But now, I was going to be her boss.

"It must have slipped her mind," I said with a smile. "How many people are in the division?"

"Right now, just you and Nikki. Detective Bryant is your PD liaison. He'll work closely with you on cases, but he is not your supervisor. I am. Of course, if you have questions about investigations, he would be the one to talk to."

"Not to sound rude," I said. "But why didn't this division land in the police department instead of the parks and recreation department?"

"I fought tooth and nail to keep it here," she said. "I know how badly you don't want to carry a gun, and if it had managed to go to PD, you would have had no choice. Plus, the city officials don't want this to be another law enforcement position, per se. You'll still be a ranger when there are no crimes to investigate within the parks."

I flipped through the binder to find a slew of policies and procedures I'd have to learn. "That makes sense. Thanks for fighting for me."

"If you ever change your mind and want a gun, you can have one. Nikki is currently going through the certification to carry one herself."

I nodded. That likely wouldn't happen, but it was nice to know.

"Here are the official documents I need you to sign." She pushed a couple of papers with highlighted areas for my signature. "You will receive an increase in pay since you are now a supervisor, but it will also come with increased responsibility. I'll mentor you on the inner workings of being a supervisor, but you'll have to figure out your own supervisory persona. I can recommend some good books now that I hear you're a reader."

I finished signing the papers and nodded. "Sure, I'd love any recommendations." Overwhelmed wasn't a big enough word to explain how I felt.

"One last thing." She pulled a large duffle bag from beneath her desk. "This is for you."

On the side, it said—*Division Leader*. When I unzipped it, I found a shiny new badge, just like the one Nikki had shown Bernie. Only mine said "supervisor." Beneath the badge were three new uniform polo shirts, one hoodie, and a heavy jacket.

"You can wear whatever pants you choose, just nothing ripped or sloppy," Ursula said. "And if you need any other type of jacket, let me know."

"Where did all the funding come from for this?" I asked. "It seems like the city is always on a tight budget."

"Let's just say, PD may have had another reason for wanting this division to be under them. Most of the funding is coming from their budget." She shrugged. "It's just the way things go."

As I dug deeper into the bag, a whole slew of supplies had been added. Office necessities, notepads, pens, a big flashlight, a multi-tool, and a few other odds and ends.

"This is great," I said. "Thank you so much, Ursula."

She slid one more piece of paper across the table to me. "This is your schedule when you're not investigating a crime. Greg can make any changes with your agreement to fill holes in the ranger schedule. When you're investigating, you're on whatever time you need to solve the crime while also giving yourself time to recover. Make sure you sleep enough. Your entire team needs to watch out for one another when it comes to health. I know you like to work yourself into the ground sometimes."

"My whole team?" I asked. "As in Nikki and me?"

"You'll be able to hire additional people in the coming months," she said. "On an as-needed basis. You can also share summies with Greg."

"Thank you again," I said. "I appreciate you doing this for me. I have one last—semi-personal—question."

She nodded. "Let's hear it."

"If, say, I was to date one of the rangers, would that still violate the rules?" My heart thumped in my throat as I waited for her answer.

"Since you're technically in a different division," she said. "It wouldn't be against the rules. However, I'd caution against dating someone you work with. It never ends well."

I smiled, relief flooding through me. "Thanks. I appreciate the advice."

"It's my pleasure," Ursula said. "Now, go find that killer."

29

Antonio met me at the shop—the oversized garage that held the ranger trucks when they weren't in use, in addition to a few offices and a loft designed for the rangers as a hangout that went unused most of the time.

Shayla and I used to work out up there.

"You look great," Antonio said, hopping out of the big black Chevy ranger truck.

He scooped me up into his arms and kissed me more passionately than he ever had before. My feet weren't touching the ground, but my toes were curling inside my tennis shoes.

When he gently lowered me back to planet earth, both physically and emotionally, he opened his eyes and smiled. "I could not help myself. I have been scratching to kiss you all day."

I giggled. "Itching. You've been itching to kiss me."

He laughed. "Right, sometimes I forget the difference." The fact that he was from Italy didn't come to

158

mind much, except when he jumbled up English phrases.

"Well, I've been itching to kiss you too," I said, rising on my tiptoes and laying another gentle kiss on his lips.

He sighed as we parted.

"Do you want me to drive?" I asked.

"I suppose that depends on what type of pet you are planning on getting," Antonio said. "I am not certain I want a llama in my back seat."

"I'm not so sure I want a llama in my apartment." I shook my head. "I'm thinking maybe a fish. Or something small. I don't need to go crazy with the second pet thing."

"Why are you getting a second pet when you sound like you do not really want one?" He held the driver's side door open for me to get in.

"It's this thing I'm doing to get myself out of a rut," I said. "I saw it on that new video app."

He laughed, then closed my door and hurried to the car's other side. "I do not usually trust social media with my life, but since this seems to have brought us together, I guess I will trust it. Just this once."

I stopped and thought about that for a moment before backing out of the parking space. Had these steps actually had something to do with Antonio and me finally getting our chance together? Was this some secret universal sauce that the pretty brunette had come across?

I laughed at myself. That was ridiculous.

Unless it wasn't.

"We need to pick up some things at a decor store, too," I said. My budget had just increased with my pay increase. If I was going to have a party with all my friends,

I needed to get my place spiffed up like the video talked about for Day Four.

"I am up for whatever," Antonio said. "I just have to be at work early in the morning. Not that I am implying we will spend the night together. I am not opposed to it, but I am not expecting it either."

This was one of the few times I'd seen Antonio so nervous. He was typically so confident, bordering on cocky. This side of him was cute.

I put the car in drive and reached over to grab his hand. He glanced over at me and smiled. "I am delighted to be spending time with you."

"Me too," I said.

We started at the shelter, but the woman laughed when I asked if I could adopt a fish. Apparently, people didn't bring their unwanted fish to the shelter.

The smallest animal she could offer me was a hamster. I almost went for it until I sent a picture to my mom, and she reminded me of all the hamsters we went through when I was a kid because they kept escaping their crazy well-built cages.

The last thing I needed was Fizzy eating my brand-new hamster.

Our second stop was a small animal store. It looked like a mom-and-pop shop, so I felt slightly okay about buying a pet rather than adopting one.

"Let's just get a fish and go," I said. "Then we can drop it off at the apartment and go shopping."

Antonio held my hand through the store as I hemmed and hawed about every fish I saw.

"I just don't feel connected to any of them," I said. "When I got Fizzy, it was instant. I knew he was my dog. But these fish all seem the same."

"They are fish, Rylie," Antonio said. "Not dogs. They do not behave the same way. A dog might wag its tail, but a fish might simply swim or pucker its lips." He made an adorable fish face.

"If you were a fish, I'd take you home," I said.

"You can take me home even though I am not a fish."

The young man behind the counter cleared his throat, and Antonio and I stepped away from each other.

"If you don't like the fish, maybe you'd like a gecko," he said in a monotone voice that made it sound like he didn't care one way or another but just wanted us out of the store.

"A gecko?" I asked. "Like a lizard?" My last encounter with Lizards had been right around my wedding. I winced at the memory.

"Geckos are super cool," the guy said. "Here, I'll show you."

He led us to a big fish tank with various tree branches and boxes inside. When he opened the top of the tank, a cute little face popped out from one of the boxes and looked right at me.

It was love at first sight.

"I'll take him," I said. "Or her."

"Her," the guy said. "But you haven't even seen her yet."

"Oh, I see her," I said. "She's amazing."

He reached in, and she crawled up into his hand. "She's a sweetheart. Here, see if she'll go to you."

I held out my hand, and she readily crawled into it, her enormous eyes still staring up at me. "I'll take her and everything that goes with her. Load me up. This is going to be the best-loved gecko in the entire world."

30

Lizzie—my brand-new leopard gecko—traveled to the apartment in her massive tank that barely fit in the backseat of my car. When Antonio and I got her through the door and onto the counter, Fizzy jumped up to meet her.

"This is Lizzie," I said. "She's hiding, but she'll be out soon. You're to make her feel welcome. Do you understand?"

He wagged his tail, so I figured he understood. Even if he didn't, it was unlikely he'd be able to get into her tank unless he desperately wanted to.

If she were a cat, I'd be worried. But being as she was a gecko, I didn't think that would make him attack quite as readily.

"Do you think we should stay for a bit and make sure she's okay?" Antonio asked.

I glanced at my phone. "We don't have much time before the decor store closes. It'll only be a few minutes."

Antonio shrugged, gave Lizzie one last look, patted Fizzy on the head, and followed me out the door.

The decor store was so overwhelming that I couldn't choose anything. There was every type of decor you could imagine. What was my style? I'd never had a style. I had my parents' style, my boyfriend's style, my fiancé's style, and even Shayla's style. Now, I had zero style at all.

Everything I picked up didn't match the last thing I'd put in my cart. I liked too many things.

Antonio stuck with me through the entire experience that ended up being worse than trying on swimsuits after a lazy winter.

When my phone lit up with a call from Nikki, I was happy to take it, if only for the distraction.

"Hello?" I said as Antonio stood off to the side of the aisle, looking at the different ridiculous signs that said things like—*Home is Where Your Butt Lands*—and—*Just Keep Swimming Lake Mode.*

He held one up that said—*I'd Rather Have Salt on My Rim than Salt in My Wounds*—and made a funny face.

I laughed.

"Rylie? Are you there?" Nikki asked from the phone.

"Yeah," I said. "What's up?"

"We found Bernie's dad," she said. "You'll never guess where he is."

I sighed. "In Colorado?"

"Ding, ding, ding, we have a winner."

"Fantastic," I said, waving for Antonio to follow me.

He motioned to the cart full of mismatched items. I shook my head. "We'll be right there."

"We?" Nikki asked. "Are you with Antonio right now?"

Heat rose in my cheeks. "Yes. I suppose he doesn't have to come with me. He probably has other things to do. I'll drop him off at his motorcycle, and then I'll be at the station."

"You little—"

"See you soon," I said, cutting her off and hanging up.

"That was Nikki," I said. "There's been a break in the case. Bernie's father is in Colorado."

"And you think they might be working together to murder people?"

I hadn't considered the possibility that Bernie made up the entire story and was working with her father to do these things. "Possibly," I finally said. "We have to do a bit more digging to find out."

"Well, I have had an incredible time with you today," Antonio said. "Could we, perhaps, do it again tomorrow?"

"Tomorrow is a prep day for the big sting since the book comes out the next day," I said. "But how about we plan on getting together after this is all figured out?"

"All my time off is yours, just like my heart."

I waited for the feeling of dread. The feeling of panic. But the only thing that moved in my chest were butterflies.

I reached over and grabbed his hand as I turned onto the road leading to the reservoir.

When we reached the shop, he leaned over and gently kissed me. "I will think about you all night. Not in a creepy way," he added quickly.

I laughed.

"Be safe."

"I will," I said. "See you soon."

As I drove back out of the park toward the police station, a squeal pushed out of my chest through my smiling lips. Was this really happening? Was I actually falling for Antonio?

31

Nikki and Harry sat in a room with a whiteboard on one wall and a long table with around ten chairs circling it.

"You found him?" I asked.

Harry pushed a photo toward me. "Herman Herrigarta traveled from England to the United States two months ago. He flew into Denver International Airport, but we cannot track his whereabouts past that. All we know is his arrival corresponds almost perfectly with the start of the murders."

I slid the photo closer to me. "What's that on his neck?" It was a rather grainy photo from a high-angle security camera.

Harry slid another photo across the table. "It could be some kind of birthmark."

"Or a tattoo?" I asked.

He glanced at me. "It could be a tattoo."

I looked between the two pictures. "I've seen this guy —the tattoo—before."

Nikki's head shot up to look at me. "Where?"

"At the strip club," I said. "He was at the bar when we got there. He's the one Percy kicked out and told to stay away from her. I assumed Percy was talking about one of the dancers, but what if it was Bernie? I think we need to make another visit to the strip club."

This time, Harry came along with us. We agreed he might get more out of Percy, being a man, than Nikki and I had.

The sun wasn't even below the horizon, but the club was already in full swing. It was busier now that it had been at midnight when Nikki and I had come last.

When we walked in, one of the dancers spotted us with a look of terror on her face.

I tried to give her a reassuring smile, but within seconds, two bouncers appeared out of nowhere and started pushing us out the doors.

"You're not welcome in this establishment," one said.

Harry and Nikki simultaneously pulled out their badges to show them, and I half wished I'd have brought mine with me, too. How cool would that have been?

"We need to speak with Percy," Nikki said. "Either he can talk to us willingly, or we can arrest him."

"Shit, the cops are here," one of the guys who had been waving a twenty-dollar bill in front of a long-legged brunette screamed.

The entire club erupted in chaos.

The bouncers tried to calm everyone down, but by the time the dust had settled, the dancers were gone, the patrons were gone, and the only people left standing in the room were the three of us, the bouncers, and the bartender.

"Never fail to make a scene, do you ladies?" the bartender asked, shaking his head at us.

"We need to speak with Percy," Nikki repeated.

"I'm right here," Percy said, coming out from the back. "I will happily speak with you if you get out of my club."

"It's not illegal to be at a strip club," Harry said. "Why was everyone running?"

"Hell, if I know," Percy said. "Guilty consciences? Not up to me to care about their personal morals. My goal is to give them a little slice of fun."

"Does that include drugs and prostitution?" I asked.

Percy seemed slightly surprised by that statement. "Look, what the girls do on their own time is their business. I am not their pimp and don't allow drugs in my establishment. Is that why you came out here and scared away all my customers? To ask about the ladies' extracurricular activities?"

"Not exactly," Harry said. "We need to talk with you about your ex-wife's arrest. And about her father's presence in your club a couple of nights ago."

The moment Harry said father, I could tell Percy was about to run.

Before he stepped in the other direction, I grabbed the front of his shirt.

Things moved quickly as he tried to tug away from me but ended up lying on the sticky floor with a ripped shirt and cuffs on his wrists.

"Hey, you can't arrest me. I did nothing wrong," Percy said, his cheek pressed against the black linoleum.

"Then why were you about to run away from us?" Nikki asked, pulling Percy to a stand with his hands behind his back. She'd gotten good at the police work side of things.

"Percy?" A high-pitched voice echoed through the empty room.

I looked around to find a woman in a short leather mini skirt and a white button-down shirt tied just below her enormous boobs. She was probably only about five-foot-tall, but with her five-inch heels, she was only a couple of inches shorter than me.

"What are you doing to him?" Her voice was full of emotion. "He hasn't done anything wrong. He runs a clean establishment here."

"Who are you?" Harry asked.

"Don't give them any information," Percy spat.

She looked from him to Harry and back again. "I don't know why it matters. I've done nothing wrong, either. We've done nothing wrong." She turned to Harry. "I'm Hattie Strickland, Percy's fiancée."

"You used to work for Bernie, right?" I asked.

Flames seemed to rise in her eyes. "Why do you want to know that?"

"Can we all go somewhere we can talk like civilized adults, please?" Nikki asked. "We're not here to accuse you of anything. We're simply trying to solve a few cases."

"I thought Bernie killed those men," Hattie said. "I saw you arrest her on TV."

"If you uncuff me, we can go into my office and chat," Percy said.

Nikki looked at Harry and then me for approval. It was the first time she'd recognized my authority.

Harry and I both nodded, but it was apparent we were all on our toes, ready to pounce.

Thankfully, Percy didn't run. He and Hattie walked hand-in-hand through the back doors into a hallway that looked like any other office building. It was a shock it was attached to the main club room.

Percy knocked on a couple of doors as we walked by, and dancers popped their heads out.

"Get back out there," he said. "The night has just begun. These officers are here to talk to me and have no interest in you."

I didn't refute his statement, but if we needed corroboration of his whereabouts during the murders, we most likely would need at least some of them to talk to us.

That was an issue for another moment.

This moment was about figuring out what the heck was going on. And fast. Time was ticking down to that release.

32

Percy's office was incredibly tidy and free of clutter. A leather couch sat at one end, and a couple of chairs were pushed up to his desk on the side opposite, where it looked like he usually sat in a bigger office-style chair.

He and Hattie sat on the couch while Nikki and I turned the chairs around to face them. Harry stood.

"Can you tell us how you know Herman Herrigarta?" I started.

"I don't know him," Percy said. "He came into the club that night you two came in. It was the first time I'd seen the guy in person."

"You'd seen photographs before?"

"When we started dating, Bernie showed me a photo of him and told me to promise I'd tell her if I ever saw him in person. Bernie was all about her promises."

Hattie gave a small grunt in agreement, and I made a mental note to return to that.

"He's a bad dude," Percy continued. "I'd bet he has something to do with those crimes."

"Why was he in your club?" I asked.

"He came in to introduce himself," Percy said. "He thought Bernie and I were still together. He said something like he wanted to make things right with her."

"And what did you say?" I asked.

"I told him we were divorced and that he wasn't welcome in my club," Percy said. "Didn't stop him from staying at the bar the rest of the night. At least we made some money off him."

"Did you tell Bernie you'd seen him?" I asked.

He turned to Hattie with an apologetic look, then back to me. "A promise is a promise. I told her I'd let her know if I ever saw him. Didn't think divorce took away that responsibility."

If Bernie knew her father was in town, why hadn't she told us? Unless they genuinely were working together. Which meant the murders would likely take place regardless of whether Bernie was in jail or not. In fact, it would make Bernie look even better in the public eye if she was in jail because then she'd be a sort of victim herself.

"Do you think Bernie could have worked with her father to commit the murders?" I asked.

Percy didn't look at Hattie this time before shaking his head. "I don't. She was terrified of him."

Hattie dropped Percy's hand and stood up.

"Come on, baby," Percy said. "You and I both know how her father killed her mother right in front of her."

"Do we?" Hattie yelled. "Do we really? Where's the proof? Bernie demanded we follow all her rules and promises, but what did she ever do for us? Nothing. She paid me less than minimum wage. She was horrible to you. Horrible to me. Horrible to everyone."

"Horrible enough to kill?" I asked Hattie.

"In my opinion, yes," Hattie said, and Percy gasped. "It's my opinion. I'm still allowed to have those, right?"

"You seem to have a very strong opinion about this," Nikki said. "Can you tell us why?"

Hattie was pacing the room in her heels with more poise than I thought was possible in such shoes. "She made me sign this big form when I started working for her about how I could only use the bathroom at certain times and couldn't talk about anything that went on in her house. Not even to Percy."

"Did something happen in her house that would lead you to believe she's capable of these murders?" Harry asked, his voice calm and reassuring.

"Did you see the garage? You had to have seen the garage. It was full of weapons."

"Those were just for research," Percy said.

"Stop defending her," Hattie yelled, her voice so shrill my eardrums felt like they might burst. "She forced me to clean up after her stupid little dogs every time they shit on the floor. And if she could still smell shit when I was done cleaning, she'd make me scrub the entire floor on my hands and knees with a toothbrush. She loves the power she has over people. Maybe she did grow up with a horrible father, but that doesn't mean she needed to turn into him. And when you told her you were leaving her for me, she almost killed you."

All three of us turned to look at Percy.

"She didn't almost kill me," Percy said. "Not intentionally."

"She threw a knife at your head."

"And missed."

"What if she hadn't?"

"It's not like she went after you when she missed. Or tried again," Percy said. "She was mad. She threw the knife, then fell to the floor sobbing. She wasn't trying to kill me."

"You know what, I'm finished with you," Hattie said, pulling off the diamond ring. "If you can't see what a monster she was, we'll never work out."

"Hattie, don't do this," Percy said. "I love you."

"Do you need anything else from me?" Hattie asked me.

I glanced at Harry and Nikki, who both shook their heads.

"Great." She dropped the ring on the ground and stormed out of the room.

Percy stood, but Harry pushed him back down to the couch. "We're not quite done with you."

"I have to go after her," Percy said. "She's the best thing that ever happened to me."

"Tell us where you were on the nights of the murders," Nikki said, listing the dates one by one.

"May I look at my calendar?" Percy said when she was finished. "It's right there on my desk."

I reached behind me, picked up the spiral-bound notebook with the word calendar on the front, and handed it to him.

He opened it to the first date Nikki had mentioned.

"I was at the club from two in the afternoon until four in the morning on the first evening. Can you tell me the others again?"

Nikki went through them one by one, and for each one, he had a solid alibi.

"My staff can confirm my whereabouts, but I also have cameras that show the parking lot," he said. "You are welcome to the footage to see my comings and goings."

"We'll definitely need that," I said. "Can you tell us any more about the encounter with Herman?"

Percy shook his head. "He came in, asked about Bernie, and then sat at the bar the rest of the night. I ended up having to kick him out when we closed."

33

At the station, in the meeting room, we went over everything in the case.

"Every man who was murdered dated this fake Henrietta from the Just Personalities app," Nikki said. "Meaning that the police officer would have too. Any luck with the company providing us with her other date information?"

Harry shook his head. "They refused. They said they were declining to abide by the warrant and that we could take them to court."

"Great," I said. "So that's a dead end, other than we know whoever is doing this has access to Bernie's house."

"Percy's looking like he's in the clear," Nikki said. She'd been going through all the footage Percy had sent to us on her laptop.

"What about Hattie," Harry said. "Though I don't know that she's capable or strong enough."

"Plus, she's with Percy almost constantly," Nikki said. "She goes in and comes out with him every single time."

"She wasn't with him when he came out the night we were there," I said.

"Maybe he sent her away when he saw Herman at the bar," Nikki said. "If he thought Herman was a bad guy, he'd probably want to protect her. I'll see what happens when I get there."

"I guess there's Herman, but since Bernie upped security, I'd guess he didn't have access to her house." I groaned in frustration. "We have to be missing something."

"Maybe Herman was working with someone who worked there," I said. "Bernie said she employed a lot of people to keep the place running, but this would have to be someone who is consistently there. Like a security guard. Or . . ."

"An assistant," Nikki said.

"June?" Harry asked.

"I mean, she has access, but does she have a motive?" I asked. "She's protective of Bernie—they go way back. Everything she's done has been to help Bernie's career."

"Maybe she wants to be paid more? Hattie said Bernie didn't even pay her minimum wage," Nikki said.

"With that car she drives and the designer clothes she wears?" I laughed. "I don't think she's hurting for money."

"But she did have those Band-Aids," Nikki said. "Did she ever send us information on whether those wounds were really from a dermatologist's visit?"

I searched through my phone email, and just a few hours earlier, I'd gotten the documents from June. "Right here." I handed Nikki my phone, and after she looked through it, she gave it to Harry.

"I don't think we have any evidence that June could be the one who did it," Harry said as he handed my phone back to me. "I'll see if we've made any progress finding her father or getting in touch with Uma."

When Harry left the room, Nikki said, "So, tell me about Antonio."

"I like him so much," I said. "Is it too soon?"

"Do you think it's too soon?"

"I don't know what I think," I said. "Maybe I'm just lonely. I've never lived alone before. Do you think I'm just trying to hook up with someone so I won't be alone?"

"Dude, stop," Nikki said. "You've been living alone since before Christmas. It's been almost three months."

She was right. I hadn't even thought about that. And sure, it had been hard, but I'd made it work.

"I got a new pet gecko," I said. "Her name is Lizzie. Oh, and I'm throwing a housewarming party after this is all over with, and I get everything redecorated."

"You are full of surprises, Cooper."

No one had ever called me by my last name before, but it was kind of cool.

"I think I found something," Nikki said, glancing down at her computer.

I scooted my chair over to her, and she turned the screen so I could see it.

"This is the night we visited the club," she said. "See, there we are."

The camera quality was pretty good at an angle from the front door, aiming down at the door and showing part of the parking lot. My hair was slightly flat, and did I really walk like that? I'd have to work on it. I looked like a toddler on the way to the bathroom.

Nikki scrolled back in the footage. "This is when Herman arrives. It looks like he's talking to someone."

"Is there a better angle of the parking lot?" I asked. "We can't even see the car."

"You can't see our cars either," Nikki said, pointing to where our cars would have been parked off the screen.

"Why wouldn't he have a video of the parking lot?"

"Privacy, probably," Nikki said. "Plus, they only really need a video of the door and who comes in and out."

"Does whoever he's talking to come inside?"

Nikki shook her head. "It's almost like they were waiting as a getaway driver. But watch what he does when he sees the camera."

I watched as Herman—a tall and muscular man—approached the door. As he reached for the handle, he looked straight into the camera and pointed his finger at it, making it look like a gun, before moving his thumb and acting like he shot the camera—or whoever was watching it.

"He's our guy," I said. "I can feel it."

"He had to have been working with someone, though. Someone on the inside."

"But who? And why?"

"That's the question," Nikki said. "And without finding him, we're back at square one."

34

When Harry returned to the conference room, I said, "We need to talk to Bernie about her father again. She knew he was in the country but acted like she didn't. Maybe she'll indicate whether she's working with him or knows who could be."

Harry agreed. "I'll bring her into the interrogation room. Do you want to talk to her?"

I nodded. "I'd be happy to."

The room was chilly when I walked in, sending my arm hairs reaching for the sky. I rubbed my hands over them to warm myself.

"Excuse the way I look. I was sleeping," Bernie said when she walked in, looking about the same as she usually did.

"We have confirmation that your father is in the States and is possibly working with someone who has inside access to your home," I said, skipping the small talk.

Bernie stared at me for a second before her eyes rolled

back in her head, and she flopped over onto the cold metal table.

"Oh my gosh," I said, hurrying to her side. "Bernie? Wake up."

Nikki and Harry walked in as I checked for breathing.

"She seems to have fainted," I said.

Nikki reached across the table, picked up one of Bernie's hands, and let it flop down on her face.

"Nikki!" I gaped at her.

"What?" She shrugged. "Now we know she's really passed out and not just faking it."

I sighed. Bernie would have had to have been an award-winning actor to fake passing out like that. But maybe she had been an award-winning actor. She'd been practically everything else.

It took a few minutes, but Bernie finally opened her eyes and looked around. "Oh, thank God I'm here," she said. "I just had the most horrible dream." She sat back up and met my gaze while Nikki and Harry left the room. "It wasn't a dream, was it?"

I shook my head. "I'm sorry, it wasn't. Your father is in town, and we believe he might be working with one of your employees to commit these murders."

"But who?" Bernie asked. "All my people are loyal and know the consequences of betraying me."

"Does anyone frequently go back to the guest bedroom with the flowery bedspread? That's where they kept the cell phone used to talk to the men through the dating app."

Maybe I was giving too much away, but we were up

against the clock. If she was the culprit, she'd already be able to assume we found the phone.

"It's right across the hall from the bathroom," she said. "The bathroom everyone uses."

She wasn't telling me something. I could feel it. But I couldn't put my finger on what that something was.

"Hattie and Percy broke up," I said, not knowing where that came from.

Bernie's eyes widened. "What do you mean? Why?"

"She wasn't happy that he had been visiting you," I said.

She tried to keep the smile off her face. "When did this happen?"

"Today." I paused, giving her time to think about it before dropping the bombshell. "You see, I think you already knew your father was in town. Percy already told you, didn't he?"

Her smile faded, and her shoulders slumped.

"So, was that all an act back there?" I asked. "The fainting spell?"

Bernie's only response was to sit back in her chair and cross her arms over her chest.

"It must have hurt to let your own hand slap you in the face," I said. "And it looks really bad for you if you did all that to fake alarm when you already knew he was in town."

"The alarm wasn't fake. I assure you of that. I didn't pass out because he's in town. I passed out because he's working with someone inside my home."

"Have you spoken to him?" I asked.

"No."

"Are you sure?" I leaned forward. "Because I'm starting to think your entire story is a lie. That your father didn't kill your mother. That the two of you are con artists working together to kill people like in your books for the publicity. Is that what's really happening?"

My voice echoed until the room was silent.

Finally, Bernie uncrossed her arms. "Attorney."

35

"I still can't figure out what the puzzle note meant—What's in a name? What does that even mean?"

"It seems to be an ode to Shakespeare," Harry said. "It means that naming things is irrelevant."

Nikki and I both gaped at him.

"Come on," he said. "The two of you need to read more."

"Do you think it could have something to do with the victim it was found on?" Nikki asked. "I mean, we didn't find notes on any of the other guys."

"Well, in the books, this body was the only one that had a note, too," I said. "But maybe that was supposed to be the last body. Like maybe it was a final push for the upcoming release."

"We can hope that's the case, but we can't operate like it is," Harry said.

I glanced at the clock. It was already five in the morning. We'd been working on this all night.

When a notification popped up on my phone, I almost laughed at what it said.

"What was that?" Nikki asked.

"I just got a notification about the next book in the series." I tapped the notification. "These apps are so smart in getting people to buy things." When the page loaded, my stomach sank. "We have a problem." I held the phone out for Nikki and Harry to see. "The book has already been released."

36

Nikki and Harry stared at me for a second before each took a turn looking at my phone.

"How long ago was it released?" Nikki asked.

"Probably at midnight," Harry said.

"Which means if our killer gets their hands on this early, we may have a body early too," I said.

"Not if we can help it," Harry said. "Call whoever is opening Alder Ridge this morning and make sure they're on the lookout for someone approaching the tower."

Antonio was opening the reservoir.

I took my phone back and dialed his number.

It rang several times before he answered. "Hey, you're up early."

"Or late," I said. "We've been working the case all night, and the book was just released a day early. Which means—"

"Hey, hold on, someone's slowing down to talk to me,"

he laughed. "They're definitely in the wrong place with the fancy car they're driving."

"Antonio, you need to be careful. The murderer could be—"

"Hey there." He wasn't listening to me. "What are you doing here?"

The sound of the gun blast echoed through the receiver.

I screamed. "Antonio! Oh my God, Antonio! Are you there?"

The sound of shuffling and a car speeding off sent tendrils of dread throughout my body.

"Someone shot Antonio," I said. "We need to get out there now."

"We're too far away," Nikki said. "Call dispatch and have them send the nearest officer and an ambulance."

Harry nodded. He was already making the call on his radio.

"Antonio?" I yelled into the receiver.

"Rylie," Antonio's voice was barely more than a groan. "Help."

"I'm coming," I yelled. "I'm coming."

I ran out of the conference room and through the police station doors.

When I got into Cherry Anne, Nikki was sliding in the passenger side.

"Let's go," she said.

I had never driven so fast in my entire life.

Nikki held on but didn't tell me to slow down. Her nose was buried in her phone.

"It sounded like Antonio recognized whoever shot him. He said they were in a fancy car."

"Rylie," Nikki said. "This book isn't the same one you told us about."

"What do you mean?" I turned to look at her and almost swerved off the road.

"A cop doesn't die in this book," she said. "A park ranger does."

"Shit," I said. "No, no, no. That can't be right. Are you sure?"

"You just drive," she said. "I'll keep reading."

I was having a hard time breathing. Antonio had been on that dating app—he knew the notification sound when it went off in my purse.

"Antonio was the target all along," I said. "They're probably not even in the park anymore. Whoever shot him probably already left."

"I don't think so," Nikki said.

"Why not?"

"Because there are two murders in this book," Nikki kept tapping her screen, trying to read the book as quickly as possible. "They find a second ranger dead after they find the first."

"Where do they take place?" I asked. "Where do the murders happen?"

"They find the first body at the gate," Nikki said. "And the second one . . ."

She tapped the screen, flipping pages forward and backward. I was about three miles from Alder Ridge.

"Where?" I asked.

"It doesn't say," Nikki said. "There's nothing—no

description. It just says they found them. They went into the park, saw the water, and found the body."

"In a parking lot?" I asked. "Or the beach? Or the plaza?"

"I think they left it open so they could play it by ear," Nikki said. "That way, wherever they find another ranger, they can make their kill."

"Are they both killed with a gun?"

"Yes," Nikki said. "Single shot to the head both times."

If Antonio had been shot in the head but was still talking, there was a chance he'd be okay. Maybe they'd missed since it was still basically dark outside.

My head spun with the different factors in the case. It couldn't be Bernie unless she were working with someone else. But the way Antonio greeted whoever shot him wasn't how he'd greet a fisherman. It was the way he'd greet someone he dated.

So if Bernie was working with someone, it was a woman. Or a woman and her father. It wasn't out of the question that a whole team of people was doing this.

There was only one woman I could think of who would have the power to change the manuscript. The only person who touched the computer after Bernie put in her passcode. Someone with a fancy car.

"June did it," I said. "She's the killer."

37

It all fit. June was the assistant, but she seemed to have a slightly different job, and position than Hattie had. The way she spoke to Bernie wasn't that of a lowly peon. And there was the picture of them together all those years ago.

"You think June—mousy little June—is the one killing all these men?"

"Think about it," I said, talking through my thoughts as fast as they came. "June works for Bernie but drives a nice, fancy car. Hattie said she didn't make minimum wage, so June must make way more money than Hattie if she can afford that car."

"Or she could just have rich parents," Nikki said. "Or been gifted a car."

She was referring to the two of us.

"I guess it's a possibility, but still," I said.

"So you think she has a more important role than just an assistant?"

"What's a person called who writes for writers?"

"Like a reporter?"

"No, like someone who actually writes the books and then the famous author puts their name on it," I said. "I think it's a spirit something. Spirit author?"

"Ghostwriter," Nikki said. "What if June is Bernie's ghostwriter?"

"Maybe that's what Bernie's been hiding. And the *What's in a name?* note would make sense in that instance, too."

"You think Bernie's been hiding the killer's identity just to keep from telling people that someone else writes her books for her?"

"It's possible," I said. "Or maybe she doesn't want to believe June is doing it. Or maybe June threatened her. If Bernie's as terrified of her father as Bernie seems, they may have blackmailed her to keep her mouth shut."

"But why? Why would they keep killing?"

"For the publicity." I shrugged. "I don't know. Or maybe June wanted credit for the books, and Bernie refused."

"And the guys June's choosing are the guys she's dated," Nikki said. "They probably rejected her or something. Didn't she say her alibi for the night the last guy died was that she was on a date? Did she ever send information on who her date was?"

I searched through my phone, knowing I wouldn't find anything. How had I been so stupid? She'd been under our noses the entire time.

The thought of Antonio with June was almost laughable. Not because Antonio was so gorgeous, but their personalities would have been so opposite. Her over-the-top attention to detail would have driven him insane.

"The mole," I said. "Antonio said he dated someone with a hairy mole on her knee. That's probably what June got removed."

When I turned onto the long road leading to the reservoir, I could see the lights flashing up ahead.

When we pulled up, the paramedics were loading Antonio into the ambulance on a stretcher.

"Is he okay?" I asked, bringing the tires to a halt with a squeal by pulling the emergency brake.

"He's alive but unconscious," one of them said. "We need to get him to the hospital right away."

"Are the police here?" Nikki asked.

"Two cars already went in," the paramedic said. "Are you Rylie?"

I nodded. "I am."

"Head down toward the office. They'll meet you there."

I disengaged the brake and sped off toward the plaza.

"He's going to be okay," Nikki said. "Keep positive thoughts."

I couldn't talk for the lump in my throat. Hot tears wove streams down my cheeks and off my chin. Things were just getting figured out between the two of us. They were so good. And now he'd been shot.

"Focus all that energy on finding June and Herman," Nikki said. "We can't let them shoot another one of our friends."

"That's it," I said, an idea popping into my head. "They're going to be looking for a park ranger. Antonio was the only one opening. If we tell all the other rangers to stay home, they'll have no one to kill. And as meticulous as June is, she won't settle for a police officer when she changed the book to include a park ranger."

Nikki was already on her phone, sending a text through the group chat.

My phone dinged a few seconds later.

Then responses came in, causing my phone to light up like flashing lights at a rave.

As we pulled into the office, I glanced around. June's fancy car was nowhere to be found.

"Do you think they knew they wouldn't find any other rangers, so they went looking for them?"

Nikki glanced around. "It's possible, but I have a feeling they're here. The second body in the book was found around a reservoir. It would make no sense if they went to a different reservoir to find a ranger."

We exited the car and hurried down into the plaza. I glanced up at the parking lot and noticed a silver car that matched the one Herman had entered outside the strip club.

"See the car?" I pointed it out to Nikki. "It's Herman's car."

Officers stood huddled outside the office door.

"We can't get in. We don't have the keys," one of them said.

Nikki pulled her keys from her belt and unlocked the office. I hurried to the security panel and typed in my code so the alarms wouldn't sound.

"Have you seen anything since you pulled in?" I asked.

"Just the abandoned car in the lot up there," one of the

officers said. "We have a feeling whoever it belongs to may be hiding out, waiting for their next kill."

"We believe it belongs to Herman Herrigarta," Nikki said. "A known murderer."

"He'll be waiting a while if it's a ranger he wants to kill," I said. "Nikki told the other rangers not to come anywhere near the reservoir."

"Good," another officer said. "I skimmed through the book and realized there's no location for the second body."

"We did, too," I said. "Poor writing, if you ask me."

"Or strategic," Nikki said.

She had a point, but still.

"We believe it's June—Bernie's assistant and possibly her ghostwriter—is working Herman," I said.

The officer held up a photo. "Harry sent us this security footage. Is this the guy?"

"That's him," Nikki said. "June is tiny, so she might hide pretty easily, but Herman won't have such luck. We should be able to find him."

"We're setting up search grids," the lead officer said. "If you'd like to join us, you're welcome. But without guns, it might not be terribly safe."

Nikki looked at me. I almost deferred to her opinion, but I was supposed to be the boss. "We'll hang back and let you do your jobs."

Nikki nodded in agreement.

They finalized their plans as a few more officers arrived.

Harry checked in with Nikki and me before heading

out and leading a group of officers down toward the beach.

I sat in the chair where Carmen—the office manager—usually sat and pulled out my phone to thumb through the book. Maybe there was another clue that I hadn't thought to check.

"Do you think they'll find her?" Nikki asked, peeking out the window.

"Eventually, yes," I said. "But maybe I can find something in here that could help."

I had barely finished my sentence when a bullet shattered part of a window right next to Nikki's head.

38

Nikki fell to the ground, and I did the same, my phone flying out of my hand and under a set of drawers across the room.

I glanced up at the window. None of the glass had come down onto the carpet.

"She's inside," I said, whipping around to look behind me, but saw nothing.

"How do you know that?" Nikki asked.

"The glass didn't fall in," I said. "It fell outside, meaning the bullet came from in here."

I peeked around the corner down the hall and saw a small figure standing in the shadows.

"June," I said, ducking back behind the wall. "I know it's you."

"It took you long enough." Her sickly sweet voice wafted through the air. "But I'm guessing you don't know why."

"I'll take a stab at it," I said. "As long as you don't shoot me."

She didn't reply.

"You were making a lot of money being a spirit writer for Bernie," I said.

"Ghostwriter," Nikki corrected from behind the counter where she sat hidden. I assumed she'd pushed the red button on her radio but hadn't heard her tell anyone where we were. Though they'd just left us here, so they should know.

"Right, you were Bernie's ghostwriter, making good money but getting none of the recognition. And you crave recognition. Even the men you dated didn't recognize how good they had it. Which gave you an idea." I stopped. "How am I doing so far?"

I didn't dare peek around the corner. If she didn't like what I was saying, she might just take the shot. Who cared at this point if she killed another person? She was caught.

"Not bad," June said. "Continue."

"You thought you'd work with Bernie's father—I'm guessing you sought him out—to blackmail Bernie into telling the truth about the writing. But Bernie doesn't care about people—you said it yourself. And no matter how many people you killed, Bernie wasn't budging. So, you tried to use her father as a scare tactic. That didn't work either because Bernie just upped her security detail."

"I'm the reason her fame skyrocketed," June said. "Her other books were okay, but with my touches on her new series, she became a bestseller overnight. And yet, she wouldn't give me even the slightest bit of credit. You read her copy of the book—tell me which one is better."

"Why would she give you credit?" Nikki asked. "Isn't

that basically your entire job description to *not* get credit?"

"Do you want a bullet through your skull like that idiot Italian?"

My insides twisted. "You know what? You won't be able to finish your mission. There aren't any park rangers coming to the reservoir today. There are, however, dozens of police officers who will be here at any moment to arrest you."

"Is that so?" June asked.

A split second later, an explosion rocked the entire building from the parking lot where Herman's car had been parked. Just the thought of how many officers had been in the vicinity made my insides hurt.

I cupped my hands over my ears and ducked my head but monitored the corner just in case June used this moment to attack.

My ears were still buzzing when June said, "Plus, last I knew, the two of you were park rangers."

39

How had I not remembered we'd told June we were park rangers the first day we met her at the coffee shop?

"We're not actually park rangers, you know?" Nikki said, her voice strange. Had she been hit by the bullet or the glass? I couldn't risk trying to see.

"Well, we all know that's a lie," June said. "You are the ones who had the keys to the building and the code. Though you didn't have to punch it in, it was already disabled."

"How did you get in?" I asked.

"Sleeping with the right guys," she said. "That Italian definitely had one thing going for him, and I'm not talking about the motorcycle."

Antonio had slept with her?

"Did I leave you speechless? If it's any consolation, I know he liked you. He talked about you on all our dates. Yes, dates plural. You probably thought he saw ugly old me and tossed me to the side, huh? Well, he didn't.

Apparently, he really was looking for love. Too bad, in the end, he was just like the rest of them."

If only the police would come.

"Nikki, you okay over there?" I finally asked.

Nikki didn't respond.

"Did you shoot her?" I asked June.

"I shot the window," June said. "It's not her I want. It's you. You're the reason Antonio dumped me. He said he could see us together, then you came into the picture, and I was out."

"Nikki," I said. "Please answer."

Panic flooded my brain. I couldn't lose Antonio and Nikki at the same time. I couldn't lose either of them. They were my only friends left.

"If you killed her, you're going to wish you were dead," I said.

"Such big words from a woman who refuses to carry a gun," June said, her voice taunting.

Anger rose within me. This woman was on my last nerve.

"You know, guns are one of the best types of weapons."

"I have no problem with guns," I said.

"Then you really should carry one." June shifted her position. "It would make situations like this slightly more fair."

"You're right. This situation isn't fair," I said. "But I'm not the one at a disadvantage. You are."

"How do you figure?"

I thought about my plan. It was stupid, but I didn't

care. She was going to shoot me one way or another. If I could stop her, maybe I'd save a few lives in the process.

"You're doing this for fame and glory," I said. "Maybe a bit of jealousy."

"Mmm-hmm."

"I'm doing this out of pure rage," I said.

"Rage?" She laughed. "You've only been dating Antonio a couple of days. How could you feel rage? You weren't even going to come back to the reservoir. You were going to walk away from all your friends."

I didn't respond. Every word she spoke, I slid closer to where she was around the corner. She'd have the perfect angle to shoot me dead if she moved.

But if she moved, I'd grab her leg and yank it out from under her.

"Oh, now you don't want to talk to me. Did that rage consume you and do my job for me?"

I was almost to the corner, my belly sliding across the tiled floor.

"Rylie Cooper, answer me," June said. "If you don't, I'll come out and kill you and your friend."

Those were the last words I needed.

I reached around the corner, grabbed her ankle, and tugged as hard as possible.

June screamed, and I used the moment of surprise to tackle her the rest of the way to the ground.

I grabbed her arms and pinned them above her head so she wouldn't shoot me with the gun. But she was stronger than I thought.

"Didn't expect that, did you?" June asked. "Wanna know a little secret?"

I didn't reply. My focus was entirely on keeping her from shooting me.

"I didn't need Herman's help to kill any of those men—sure, he was helpful with the barrel. But when he tried to jump on *my* bandwagon—stalking around the club, making threats—I did to him what I did to all the others."

Even with all my body weight sitting on her legs and holding down her arms, she was slowly moving from beneath my grasp. I needed to get the gun before it was aimed at me again.

"If there are any officers left after that explosion," she said, taunting me, "they'll find him scorched in his trunk. He was scorched before the explosion. I'll have to write that in the next novel."

She'd be writing that novel from prison if I had anything to do with it.

"Getting tired yet?" she asked. "Your arms are shaking. You're not exactly in ranger shape anymore, are you? Must be all those snacks while reading mystery novels."

How much had Antonio told her about me?

I had to do something quickly. My only option was to let go of one of her arms and reach for the gun. She was right. I was out of shape. But my life depended on this.

I let go and reached, but I was too slow.

The gunshot went off, and blood went everywhere.

I fell backward off of her, waiting for the pain to hit. For the darkness to take over.

Was this what it was like to die? I had to be dead. Or numb. Or in shock.

There was so much blood, but I didn't feel a thing.

"Get up." Nikki's voice came from above me.

I opened my eyes to see her holding a hand out for me to grab.

When I looked back at June, it was apparent what had happened.

Nikki shot her.

The blood was June's blood, not mine.

I took Nikki's hand and came to a stand. "I didn't think you were allowed to carry a gun yet."

Nikki shrugged. "You gonna fire me, boss?"

"Not a chance in the world."

She wrapped an arm around my shoulders and hugged me to her side. "Let's get to the hospital."

40

Antonio was just coming out of surgery when we arrived. The police delayed us at the scene for far longer than I thought was necessary, but they needed to get everything documented for their reports. Nikki and I also got some things documented because I'd have reports of my own to fill out when all of this was over.

The nurses wouldn't let us go back to see him until it was almost evening, and he was stable.

When I came to his side, I grabbed his hand in mine and let the tears stream down my face.

He was unconscious but breathing on his own. The doctor told us he was incredibly lucky, and as long as there weren't any additional complications in his healing, he should be able to return to his former self in time.

"I'm here," I said. "I'll be here as long as I need to be. I'm not leaving your side."

Of course, I couldn't keep that promise because the

nurses only let me stay with him for a little over a half hour before they told me to come back in the morning.

Nikki met me in the waiting room. "How is he?"

"He has a bandage wrapped around his head, and his face is a bit swollen, but otherwise, he looks like himself."

"I'm so sorry this is happening," she said.

"Me too."

"Does this change your mind about coming back?" Her voice was so fragile. It was the least confident I'd ever seen her.

"Not in the slightest," I said. "In fact, it makes me want to come back even more so we can keep things like this from happening in the future."

"Are you going to get a gun?" Nikki asked.

I shook my head. "I'll trust you to take care of that side of things."

She pulled me into a hug. "I hope it's okay. I'm hugging my boss."

I wrapped my arms around her and pulled her closer. "Any time."

I drove home, ready to snuggle up with Fizzy and Lizzie and watch TV. My time reading mystery novels was probably over for a while. I understood why Harry stuck to romance.

When I pulled into my parking space, my jaw nearly dropped open.

Luke stood on the sidewalk holding a massive bouquet of flowers and a huge smile.

I got out of the car, and the first thing he noticed was the bloodstains still on my shoes.

"What is all that?" he asked. He put the vase of flowers on the ground and gathered me into a hug. "Are you okay?"

"It's been a long day," I said, unsure what to do. Antonio—the guy I'd been dating—was in a hospital bed, and the guy I'd wanted to date until a few days ago stood in front of me. He was supposed to be in the Middle East. Not here, comforting me.

I pulled away and bent down to pick up the flowers. "I assume these are for me?"

He gave me a disappointed look. This was obviously not how he expected his homecoming to go. "Yeah, they're for you."

"They're beautiful," I said, trying to smile at him. "Let's go upstairs and talk."

He nodded and followed me silently up to my apartment.

When I opened the door, the first thing I noticed was Fizzy hopping around like a crazy dog. He probably had to pee something fierce.

The second thing I noticed was the change in my apartment.

"Whoa, I see someone decorated," Luke said. "It looks great. Very you."

It was very me. But I hadn't decorated.

I glanced around at all the new pictures and decorations, but the moment my eyes landed on a sign that said —*I'd Rather Have Salt on My Rim than Salt in My Wounds*—I knew exactly who had decorated.

"There's a card here for you," Luke said. "Sorry, I read it before I realized . . ."

He handed me a simple notecard.

I hope you like it. You deserve a home that's as lovely as you are. Yours, Antonio

"Seems things have changed since I left," Luke said.

I looked up at him with tears in my eyes. "Antonio was shot. He's in the hospital."

"And the two of you were . . ."

"Dating," I said. "I don't know. It was new."

"I see." Luke walked over to Lizzie's cage and looked inside.

"What are you even doing here? You said you were going to be gone for months."

"They pulled everyone out of the Middle East," he said.

"Who did?"

"The President," he said. "Do you not watch the news?"

I shook my head. "I've been reading mysteries. It's a long story."

"Does all of this have something to do with the blood on your shoes?"

"It does," I said. "But can we talk about it another time? I'm so tired, and I just can't do this right now."

"I guess I thought you'd be more excited that I'm staying."

"I am," I said. "It just hasn't sunk in yet."

"I'll come back tomorrow," Luke said, bending down for a kiss.

I turned my head, and his lips landed on my cheek.

When he returned to a stand, his gorgeous face turned into a frown.

"I'm sorry, Luke. I didn't—"

He put a finger to my lips. "Shhh. We'll talk about it tomorrow. Get some rest."

I nodded, and he leaned down and kissed the top of my head.

"I'm glad you're home," I said.

He looked back one more time before walking out the door. "I'm glad to be home . . . I think."

When the door clicked into place, I slid down onto the couch. Fizzy crawled up in my lap as tears of confusion, grief, and indecision slid down my face into his fur. "What am I going to do, Fizz?" I looked around my apartment and couldn't help the smile on my face. It was wonderful. Antonio had done such a good job—a much better job than I could have done myself.

Then my mind went to Luke. The man I'd waited years for. The man who had swept me off my feet the moment I was left at the altar, only to leave me a few weeks later.

"What am I going to do?"

· · ·

Thank you so much for reading *Booked*! If you could share it with your friends, review on Goodreads/Amazon/Bookbub, or post about it on social media, I would be so thankful!

· · ·

Read the next book in the Rylie Cooper Series—*Signed!*

Join my newsletter for updates and exclusive content!

ACKNOWLEDGMENTS

I wrote this book in the midst of a particularly sad time in my life. It amazed me how writing ended up being so therapeutic, even though I wasn't writing about what was happening.

I considered dedicating this book to sweet and spunky Makenna who was taken from this world far too early, but I just couldn't come to terms with dedicating a murder novel to someone who had so recently passed away. Therefore, I want to make a note here for Makenna.

Every time I see a sunset, I think of you. I know you're in a better place where there's no pain, but we miss you and love you so much. Thank you for giving so many people so many wonderful memories. Until we meet again . . .

Of course, I'd also like to thank all of my friends, family, arc readers, beta readers, and reader readers! Thank you, God, for giving me a creative outlet for my pain.

ABOUT THE AUTHOR

Stella Bixby is a native Coloradan who loves to snowboard, pluck at the guitar, and play board games with her family. She was once a volunteer firefighter and a park ranger, but now spends most of her time making up stories and trying to figure out what to cook for dinner.

Connect with Stella on Facebook, Twitter, and Instagram @StellaBixby.

Stella loves to hear from her readers!
www.stellabixby.com

ALSO BY STELLA BIXBY

Novels:

Rylie Cooper Series

Catfished: Book 1

Suckered: Book 2

Throttled: Book 3

Tampered: Book 4

Whacked: Book 5

Bungled: Book 6

Snowed: Book 7

Wasted: Book 8

Booked: Book 9

Shayla Murphy Series

Mistletoe Malarkey: Book 1

Veiled Vengeance: Book 2

Magical Mane Mystery Series

Downward Death: Book 1

Bowling Blunder: Book 2

Spotlight Scandal: Book 3

Tango Trouble: Book 4

Spelunking Speculations: Book 5

Festival Fiasco: Book 6

Jamboree Justice: Book 7